# The Iron Cobweb

# THE IRON COBWEB

## Ursula Curtiss

Thorndike Press • Chivers Press
Thorndike, Maine USA   Bath, England

BC mт B·M NW

This Large Print edition is published by Thorndike Press, USA
and by Chivers Press, England.

Published in 1999 in the U.S. by arrangement with
Brandt & Brandt Literary Agents, Inc.

Published in 1999 in the U.K. by arrangement with
John Curtiss III.

U.S.  Hardcover  0-7862-2152-6   (Mystery Series Edition)
U.K.  Hardcover  0-7540-3998-6   (Chivers Large Print)

The text of this Large Print edition is unabridged.
Other aspects of the book may vary from the original edition.

Set in 16 pt. Plantin by Rick Gundberg.

Printed in the United States on permanent paper.

**British Library Cataloguing-in-Publication Data available**

**Library of Congress Cataloging-in-Publication Data**
Curtiss, Ursula Reilly.
   The iron cobweb / Ursula Curtiss.
    p.    cm.
   ISBN 0-7862-2152-6 (lg. print : hc : alk. paper)
   1. Large type books.  I. Title.
  [PS3505.U915I75  1999]
  813'.54—dc21
                                         99-43304

# The Iron Cobweb

# 1

When had she begun to feel afraid? Now, this instant, in this tiny shocking part of a November afternoon? Or a day, a week, a month ago, her brain hiding its own uneasy knowledge in a deep-down layer that consciousness didn't plumb?

Elizabeth March didn't know, then or later, but she always remembered that crisp shuddery day. Branches restless against the sky, a threat of snow on the air. Her own long spacious comfortable living-room, walled in misty grey, curtained in red and green and white striped linen, firelit. The hands on the gilt wedding-present clock, miraculously preserved through five years, pointing to four o'clock. And, close and clear, the sound of a baby crying.

She was on her feet instantly, wrenching the front door open on the icy air. The sounds were unmistakable now, small mewings followed by loud miaowing wails. Elizabeth ran down the steps between cedars and found the source: three and a half year old Maire, snow-suited in navy blue, lying nonchalantly back in her wagon and mimicking at the sky.

Relief — and that was frightening in itself — turned to anger. "Maire!" she said sharply. "Stop that at once. What in the world do you think you're doing?"

The child tilted upright, pale curls that looked like chiffon escaping wildly from under the navy helmet. "That's my baby," she said, her voice as severe as Elizabeth's. "My baby cries all the day long."

She wasn't far removed from a baby herself; hang on to that. "Tell her from me," said Elizabeth weakly, "that she'll have to go up to her room if she's going to make all that racket."

She left Maire scolding talkatively at the empty air; she went back up the steps and turned just in time to see Noreen Delaney, the children's young nursemaid, rounding the corner of the house, her cheeks rosy with cold, her voice full of reproach. "Maire Ann March, I thought you were a nice big girl. Here's poor little Jeep been looking for you, but he thought it was a baby on the lawn and not his sister. . . ."

She caught sight of Elizabeth then, and permitted herself a smile and an anxious, "You'll catch your death without a coat, Mrs. March.

8

I thought I might pull them once around the block in their wagon before supper."

"Don't get too cold yourself," said Elizabeth.

"Oh, we're all mittened. In you go, Jeep. . . ."

Jeep, John Paul when he attained the age of dignity, climbed laboriously into the red wagon. At two, Elizabeth thought, watching, it must be quite a hazardous feat. He accomplished it safely, Maire shouted, "Take good care of my baby, Mama," Noreen turned for a smile and a wave and they were gone, down the lawn and under the trees and behind the high privet hedge.

Elizabeth, shivering, went back to the fire. She wasn't really aware of physical cold; the chill was deep and inner. She blamed herself for her annoyance at Maire; the child was — what would the specialists call it at fifteen dollars an hour? — compensating. And Jeep too, very possibly, because who knew what went on behind the wide wondering eyes of a two-year-old boy? They heard talk about doctors and hospitals and a baby and apparently understood nothing, but when Elizabeth left in that white rigid hush, to be gone two weeks, they expected her to return with a baby.

And so did I, thought Elizabeth leadenly, and so did I.

Skip that, skip with every ounce of mental strength the thing that happened daily to thousands of women — the pain, the confusion, the submission; afterwards the serene and lazy wonder: a sister for Maire, or a boy to bounce and tumble with Jeep? And then her doctor at her bedside instead of a nurse; instinct told her the meaning of that, the dreadful final meaning. She still had to listen to his voice, ruffled out of its expensive calm, telling her that she must be brave, that she must think of the other children. . . .

Extraneous, all of it, because that was six weeks ago and she was well again. She had rested obediently and swallowed quantities of capsules, and allowed herself to be caught up again in the hair-raising pace set by two small children. There were still the nights, long, merciless, loud with the things that Oliver, her husband, would not say. That if she had listened to him, if she had not been so illogically insistent upon flying to New York for the wedding of a friend, her accident on the way to join him at the airport could never have happened.

If he had said it, if he had not turned his head away so sharply when she tried to say it, its echoes would have died away between them before this.

But it was the days that you lived and gradually the sense of loss had dulled; little by little Oliver's face had lost its quietly frantic look. After a while, with the help of a new nurse for the children and the efficient presence of a cousin temporarily-turned-housekeeper, it was almost as though the months of waiting and the final failure had never been.

Except that there was something wrong, something as delicate and disturbing as motion sensed out of the corner of the eye. And it was this that made Elizabeth afraid.

Somewhere in the house, branches scraped against a window. The wind was sharpening . . . were the children warm enough? But Noreen had said just around the block; they'd be back at any minute. Elizabeth left the hearth and crossed the room to the round gilt mirror and looked deliberately at herself.

The glass distorted, and gave back a humblingly small image. Black cashmere, ringed at the throat with a strand of snowy buttons. Small creamy face above it, still a little too hollow in the cheeks, with hair the pale sunny colour of Maire's brushed shiningly close to her head. Indeterminate eyes — blue? green? — too wide in concentration under surprisingly dark brows.

Afraid? asked Elizabeth of the searching eyes. Afraid of what?

11

Nothing she could face. Like the motion caught or imagined in the tail of the eye, the uneasiness hid when she looked for it. Or, rather, it took on the colour of any circumstance, like a defensive animal finding protection, so that it might be concealed in almost anything.

It might be Oliver, with his new and disconcerting habit of watching her when he thought she didn't notice. Watching almost clinically — and remembering? — so that when he would say casually, "Tired?" she marshalled her answer as carefully as though he were a visiting psychiatrist and not the man she had loved without guard for five years.

It might be Constance Ives, Elizabeth's second cousin, taking over — soothingly, quietly — any household affair requiring more thought than, say, a five-year-old child could give it. Constance, in Massachusetts on a chance visit to the cousin she hadn't met more than twice in her thirty-plus years, had been a rock in those first dream-like days after the hospital. She was a wall now, steady, reliable — and completely unassailable. Was there someone else behind the wall, someone who resented a lifetime of aprons and grocery lists, someone Elizabeth wouldn't recognize if the wall ever cracked?

Or the wrongness might be in Lucy Brent.

Why, thought Elizabeth edgily, must I be carried off to Bonwit's on shopping trips when there isn't a thing I want? Or to fashion shows, which I loathe? Or on long drives, ending up with tea at some horribly quaint place, which must bore Lucy nearly as much as they do me? Is it occupational therapy, or what?

She was ashamed of that instantly because Lucy, bound by no ties at all beyond a friendship of two years' standing, was merely doing her darting, dragonfly best to divert Elizabeth, and sacrificing, along the way, quite a few hours of her beloved high-stakes bridge. And Lucy had no children, and no recognition of children, so that she couldn't know.

Oddly enough, of them all, it was Lucy's husband whom Elizabeth had felt most at ease with in the past few weeks. Steven Brent was shy and thoughtful and often inarticulate; where her cousin Constance Ives was a rock, he was a cushion, but in the buoyant and deliberate way that a life-raft is a cushion. Of them all, it was Steven who had said openly, "I wish we could help. But you'll deal with it your own way," and had then gone on treating her as a normal, intelligent woman.

Normal.

Voices on the frosty air. Maire's: "Mama! Where are you, Mama? I found a duck!"

Jeep's, tearful: "Mine, MINE," and then an outburst of rage and sorrow. The wagon rattled, Noreen's voice threaded serenely through the altercation. Jeep's sobs quieted. Elizabeth went to the door, feeling as though she had come out of shadow into sunlight, and soberly admired a wooden duck faded from countless rains. Noreen, brisk with zippers and mittens in the lighted kitchen, nodded at the duck and said conversationally, "Expendable, I think, as soon as possible? We had to take it along to avoid a scene."

She smiled at Maire as she said it. Countless other Delaneys had obviously followed Noreen into the world, Elizabeth thought gratefully. She said, "Oh, I wouldn't worry, let them have it if they want it."

Jeep gave the duck a look of love. Maire, losing interest, put up a hand to Elizabeth's and began to pull her toward the door. Noreen said doubtfully, "They say they don't want scrambled eggs, Mrs. March. . . ."

"Oh yes they do," said Elizabeth with firmness, and caught Noreen's eye. "This is the entering wedge, I warn you. About once a month they start fancying themselves as old Romans. Put your foot down fast."

The worried look vanished from the young too-thin face. Not the twenty — two she said she was, thought Elizabeth with a momentary

14

qualm; probably not a day over twenty. But you could need a job and a home just as much at twenty as at twenty-two, and the girl was competent and seemed content. The children had taken to her instantly, and that was ninety per cent. of the battle.

The grip of Maire's hand grew more impatient, "I'll tell you a secret, Mama —"

The secret, Elizabeth knew, allowing herself to be escorted into the living-room, would be long and completely inaudible, with Maire's pink-silk cheek pressed earnestly against her own and her lips moving soundlessly.

In the instant before she sat down on the couch, Elizabeth caught a tiny sliding reflection of their two figures in the round mirror over the mantel. And the magic began to work again. How could she, how could any woman have the temerity to be afraid when her life had built itself up so beautifully around her? When she had a husband whom she loved, who loved her. Two healthy children who didn't know the meaning of fear. If no staggering wealth, at least no financial worries. And her own health, snatched out of danger six weeks ago. If that was all she had salvaged on that dreadful morning, it was still a great deal.

Any notion that things were somehow not

what they seemed, that something was nibbling softly at the base of the structure, was nonsense.

Solemnly, Elizabeth bent her cheek for Maire's secret.

"I suppose they'll want cheese and crackers with their drinks," said Constance, "or do you think sandwiches?"

"The Brents?" Elizabeth was momentarily startled, because she and Oliver had never consciously entertained Lucy and Steven. It was always more a matter of sitting around, arguing amicably, until someone, usually Oliver, said around midnight, "What's in the icebox besides the light bulb?" And then there was a general exodus into the kitchen, without the thread of the argument even trembling.

But Constance Ives wouldn't be a party to any such haphazard arrangements. The prop of an invalid mother for nearly twenty years, she had learned, along with infinite patience, that you could keep an iron-clad control of any social situation if things were arranged in advance. So many drinks, so much sustenance, offered with a sensible eye on the clock. After a suitable week or two had elapsed, you went to *their* house.

She was waiting now, eyebrows lifted a little over the pale grey eyes. The lids were thick and white and drooping, as though she were facing a strong light. Or as though, Elizabeth had thought once, Constance stored her secrets under those pale lazy folds of flesh, and you mightn't know her if she suddenly opened them wide and the secrets blazed at you.

She brought her mind back guiltily to Constance's question. "Oh — cheese and crackers, I suppose, isn't that easier?"

"It isn't a question of that," said Constance, burying a rebuke in good humour. "I wasn't sure what you usually gave them."

"Cheese and crackers," Elizabeth said mildly, zippering her dress, "because I'm lazy to begin with and it *is* easier."

Constance stood up and went slowly to the door of the bedroom, plainly wanting to say something, hesitating. Elizabeth said cheerfully, "Slip showing?" and Constance flushed and shook her pale brown head. "This is the first time you've really entertained at all since — I mean . . . do you think . . . black?"

Distantly, downstairs, Oliver clattered ice into a bucket. Constance looked distressed. Elizabeth pushed back her involuntary anger and said, "I've always worn a lot of black. Heavens, you didn't think it was mourning?"

The flush in the long face deepened to red. Constance said wretchedly, "No, I just — I

17

. . . I'll see about things in the kitchen," and fled, stumblingly.

I'll have to stop this, thought Elizabeth clearly, attaching ear-rings without looking at them. Or pretty soon I *won't* be normal. . . .

Later, the evening telescoped itself for her. There was Lucy's face, small, bony, elegant; Lucy's voice with relief under its animation: "Look at her, Steven, she's blooming. What's the penalty for malingering in this state?" There was Steven, smiling and quiet and somehow reassuring: "Of course she's blooming. She's going to do a book for us soon, aren't you, Elizabeth? Been at your typewriter yet?"

There was Constance, effacing herself expertly, giving precedence to talk and laughter just as she had given precedence to her mother's illness and medicines. Most important of all for Elizabeth, there was Oliver, taking the brunt of the evening on his own shoulders, although you could only know that if you were married to him. Oliver glancing at the clock at close to midnight, and coming across to her as quietly and intently as though there were only the two of them in the room, and saying lightly, "Off you go. Doctor's orders, at a hundred bucks a syllable."

Elizabeth hadn't felt tired until then; she realized all at once that the thin betraying dampness had started along her forehead. There were goodnights and apologies, and upstairs in their room Oliver's sudden kiss, almost angry in its intensity. "Take care of yourself, hear? I won't have you pushing our luck. Wait a minute. . . ."

He crossed the room to her bureau. Elizabeth, feeling bereft of his arms, said wearily and happily, "But I don't want a pill, darling. Honestly."

"That's what you think tonight." Oliver went briskly into the bathroom, filled a water glass and returned, holding pill and glass imperatively before her. Elizabeth laughed at him. "You don't want me to fall asleep taking off my dress? This zipper requires the clearest of heads. I'll take it when I'm in bed, and look, you'd better go down, you've been gone much too long already. . . ."

The bedroom was very peaceful: white candlewick on the beds, curly sea green rugs on the floor, toile curtains in ivory and burnt red shutting out the wild windy night. Elizabeth, prolonging the peace and the heavenly sensation of not being required to do anything at all, lay contentedly on her bed without undressing. Cigarette, shower, sleep . . .

For the first time in weeks she could laugh at herself, she could wake out of a disturbing dream to her own solid happiness. That was worth all the vitamin capsules in the world, all the sleeping pills — one of which she would presently take. . . .

She finished one cigarette and absentmindedly lighted another. In the middle of that a motor started into life down in the driveway, shouted farewells echoed on the air. After a few moments the stairs creaked and careful footsteps approached, receded. Constance.

Oliver would be coming up in a minute — or having a last brandy beside the fire. Elizabeth slid off the bed and smoothed her sheath of black. She thought, He must know I've been odd. It's only fair he should know I've come to my senses, and opened her bedroom door and went down the stairs. They could still, after five years of marriage, with two children fathoms deep in sleep in the room next to theirs, come quietly and surprisingly to each other and find all the pleasure of the beginning.

But Oliver wasn't beside the fire. She caught a glimpse of his shoulder in the glass door that led to the sunporch. The shoulder swung out of sight, as though he had bent very suddenly. Elizabeth had her hand on the knob of the door when she heard, mystifyingly, the sound of Oliver's voice. It was slow and bitter, wrenched from him. It said,

"That's all very well — and you know how much it means to me. But" — an impact as though a despairing palm had pounded down on leather — "what are we going to do about Elizabeth?"

# 2

What indeed will we do about Elizabeth?

That crossed her mind like a sword thrust and was gone, because there wasn't time now. In the immeasurably small interval between the moment she had touched the doorknob and the moment when Oliver's words had split her consciousness, the knob had turned under her fingers. And creaked.

Elizabeth pulled the door wide and stepped out on to golden rope rug. They must have sprung apart very nimbly. Lucy Brent was leaning against one of the built-in bookcases at the end of the long narrow room; Oliver, a chair away, was deadening a cigarette in an ashtray and looking up with an air of pleased surprise.

This was where experience let you down. To wake from a pleasant dream to ugly reality wasn't fair; it wasn't in the book. Elizabeth said carefully, feeling her way: "Footnote to the doctor's orders — Benedictine when wakeful. Any left?"

"Quarts." Had Lucy's breath come out in a sigh first? Examine it later, because this was quite important. Oliver said, pouring, "Here you are," and then, "You didn't take your pill."

"No . . ." How much better if she had. And how bewildering of Oliver to put it that way, half-accusingly. Or . . . how clever.

"Steven's off, he had one of those long manuscripts to finish before morning. A tome," said Lucy critically. "One of those wartime marathons. He deserted me for it last night too, but that's no reason why I should keep you people up until all hours."

"Nonsense," Elizabeth said. She felt breathless; did she sound it? Did Oliver, four feet away, sense the slow pounding of her heart? "I'm off myself. See you soon, Lucy."

It was abrupt, but it was all she could manage, setting her half-emptied glass on a table, smiling at them both, closing the door quietly behind her. She carried the same audience, invisible, up the dark stairway and into the bedroom.

*What are we going to do about Elizabeth?*

Oliver's car drove away and returned. Elizabeth, still in every nerve and muscle, listened to his footsteps as he locked doors and turned off lights and mounted the stairs. He tiptoed cautiously through the bedroom; the light went on in the bathroom and there was a violent sound of toothbrushing. When the light was finally flipped out and Oliver padded barefootedly past the end of her bed to his own, Elizabeth held herself braced under her blankets. Now wasn't the time to talk about it or even think about it; not now when she was still echoing all over with shock. She breathed shallowly over a sudden tickle in her throat, but the cough escaped.

Oliver said instantly out of the darkness, "Elizabeth?"

"Yes?" Draggingly, as though she had just surfaced from sleep.

"You're awake, I can see the whites of your eyes."

"I'm awake then. Temporarily."

There was the sound of Oliver propping himself on his elbow. "You stayed up too long. Better watch it, just at first."

Was it possible, wondered Elizabeth amazedly, that he was, as he thought, waking her in order to tell her to get more sleep? Was it even possible that he was chiding her for not having stayed where she had been tenderly put earlier that evening? She said calmly, "It was nice to have Steven and Lucy again."

"Nice couple," Oliver's voice answered idly. He withdrew the propping elbow and there was a comfortable settling sound of sheets and blankets, "Easy to take."

Easy to take.

What are we going to do about Elizabeth?

The first snow of the year began a little before dawn. Elizabeth woke to the whisper of it on the changing wind, and didn't go back to sleep. Her mind had become a sounding board; it echoed senselessly with what she had heard Oliver say to Lucy Brent the night before. "You know how much it means to me —" like a man viewing freedom from behind bars. And then the stunning, the brutally brisk query about the disposal of Elizabeth. To Lucy, which was, as if it mattered, a double betrayal.

Oliver showered and shaved and dressed at seven-thirty, making a good deal more noise than he generally did. Elizabeth lay curled on her side, her eyelashes carefully down; she would have liked to pull up the blankets against the blast of snowy air from the window, but you couldn't do that with a convincingly sound-asleep air. A tie whistled through the rack, there was a moment of concentrated silence, and Oliver crossed the room to her bedside. He hesitated. Elizabeth went on breathing neutrally and was rewarded by the sound of the door closing gently. She sat up against her pillow and lighted one of the ciga-

rettes Hathaway had forbidden before breakfast.

In the first place, there might be another explanation. (But why, then, had she had that
feeling of unease, the feeling that was almost
fear?) And if there was, wouldn't perceptive
Oliver have made it last night?

In the second place, the explanation might
be exactly what it seemed. Lucy Brent was a
thoroughly charming woman, with an odd
elusive attraction of her own. A little dissatis-
fied with her own marriage, although that was
only a guess on Elizabeth's part, because
Steven's salary as an editor in a publishing
house would never be, in all probability, as elegant as her own tastes and inclinations. Possibly, because it was true of the most
unexpected women, restless and bored with
her own childless state.

But . . . *Lucy?*

Suppose Oliver had meant exactly what he
had seemed to mean. It wasn't simple even
then, because quite apart from the problem of
Lucy and Steven, there were two whole life-
times, essenced into five years of marriage: you
gave the sum total of yourself. There were two
children who accepted love and belonging as
casually as sun and stars and breakfast. Could
you, having taught them trust, let them in for a
battle far more real and personally dangerous

than guns on the other side of the world?

Careful, thought Elizabeth. Careful.

Maire was delighted with the snow; Jeep eyed it with sophisticated calm. Elizabeth took a window-by-window tour of the house, showing astonishment because it was snowing outside the children's room as well as outside the kitchen, while Jeep sat lethargically on the floor in the living-room, mumbling over his trucks.

The firm grip of Maire's small hand in hers took on an utterly new meaning for Elizabeth. Is this, thought Elizabeth in wonder, looking down, is this in the balance?

She would have to see Lucy, of course. Casually, and in the course of friendship, but with the special perspective that knowledge gave. When she had done that, and when she had seen Oliver and Lucy together again, she would know better what to do.

Constance was having breakfast in the dining-room, consuming toast and damson jam with the detached and delicate greed that had always fascinated Elizabeth. She made a point of breakfasting after Oliver, as though to spare him the inflaming sight of food, his food, being put to use. Oliver had once said annoyedly, "Does she think I'm going to whip it out from under her nose, or what?" And

Elizabeth had answered soberly, "Some people, you know, keep an eagle eye on the pantry. Aunt Kate was quite capable of it. Leave her alone, she likes it better that way."

She said now, "More coffee, Constance, when I get mine?" and Constance tucked in a last buttery crumb with precision and put down her napkin and started to rise. "I'll get it, Elizabeth, you sit down." As though, thought Elizabeth with a new edge of irritation, the modest salary she had forced upon her cousin turned her into a servant, caught relaxing. She said, "Stay where you are, I'll get it," and went into the kitchen.

Noreen Delaney, assembling boots and mittens while the children waited expectantly, glanced up. "Good morning, Mrs. March. Isn't it lovely? I thought I'd teach them fox-and-geese while the snow's still fresh, if they don't get too wet at it."

"They will; that's a game by itself," Elizabeth said, smiling. "Don't let them wear you out."

The coffee was still hot; she gave it an extra minute over the gas and poured two cups. Maire, absorbed in the legs of her snowsuit, said in a sweet absent voice, "Don't wear me out, Jeep, you know you mustn't wear me out."

"Parrot," said Elizabeth, and to Noreen,

"I'll be out very shortly to take over myself."

Why had she said that? Because of a natural impulse to share the first snow with her children? Or because, with danger hanging over all their heads, she wanted to scoop up all the love she could?

The kitchen door closed behind them, their voices began to flute excitedly on the air. In the dining-room Constance said, "You look rather pale, Elizabeth. I hope last night wasn't too much for you — how did you sleep?"

How did I, indeed? But she had. The body would take only so much from the mind. "Very well," said Elizabeth. "How about you?"

"Oh, quite well, as usual. I did think," Constance wrinkled her brow, "that I heard a car go out after the Brents left. I started to wonder if something was wrong, and then I fell asleep."

Her tone dropped the matter there, but the pale eyes under the heavy lids took it up again, speculatively. Elizabeth retreated behind her coffee cup and said over the rim, "Oh, that's right — Steven had a manuscript to read. Lucy had hopes of winning an argument from Oliver, I gather, so she stayed a while."

"And did she?" Constance was bland, folding her napkin. "Win, I mean?"

She knew.

She doesn't, thought Elizabeth, angry at herself; she can't possibly. She's shrewd, but she isn't radar. She put down her coffee cup and shook her head. "You'd have to ask Oliver — I was too drugged to bother. Is there anywhere you'd like to go this morning . . . ?"

At three o'clock the house was empty of everyone but herself, and too still.

The children, bundled and booted like miniature paratroopers, had trudged off for a walk with Noreen, who seemed to find a pleasure almost equal to theirs in the fresh white world. Constance had taken the car into the village to treat with Mr. Willet, the grocery manager, over the matter of a roast. There was no word from Lucy Brent, who had said something about an auction the night before.

Would a house, or at least your own pleasant familiar house, seem so empty if there weren't a corresponding hollowness inside? At a quarter to four, because the walls seemed to be closing in, Elizabeth put on her boots and coat, left a brief note on the kitchen table and went out into the frozen stillness.

Fox and geese tracks in the snow, blurry imprints where the children had made angels — don't get maudlin, she told herself crisply, and went on her way. The March property was large, by current real-estate standards:

30

nearly three acres that in summer turned into lawn and borders, a wooded hillside, a raspberry patch, a grape arbour. And at the top of the hill, built with abandon when Elizabeth sold her first book, the studio.

She hadn't been here since her return from the hospital. The key was still under the single wooden step. Elizabeth unlocked the door and didn't close it behind her because the air was heavy with damp and disuse. Her eyes went at once to the typewriter beside a window; it was somehow weird that the same sheet of yellow copy paper should still be there, waiting timelessly for the end of a sentence.

Sprigged chintz at the three windows, a day-bed where she'd slept more than once, an overflowing bookcase, an armchair: it was a comradely room, remote enough to be in another world. Her glance stopped on a black glass corkscrew of lamp, topped with a cone of gold straw. Lucy had given her that. She had a sudden childish impulse to fling it out the open door and into the snow.

"Elizabeth?"

For an instant, staring at the closed door that led into the lavatory, Elizabeth didn't breathe. Then someone said her name again, behind her, and Steven Brent's head appeared in the open doorway. "No editors allowed, I know, but I brought back some books of yours and saw your note. Thought I'd drop by and ask whether we laid you low last night."

What inspiredly unhappy phrasing, thought Elizabeth, and made the appropriate denials. "Come on in — or don't, it's freezing. Come back to the house and have some sherry."

"Thanks, but I can't stay."

Nevertheless, he didn't go at once. He said he would like to have Elizabeth meet the president of Hornham's, his publishing house, for lunch one day soon; could he go ahead and arrange it? Elizabeth said yes, vaguely. She had an odd notion, probably groundless, that this wasn't what Steven had come to say at all, that something had changed his mind.

They talked for the space of a cigarette, and because he was the person with whom Elizabeth felt easiest now her mind could free itself and go off on a path of its own. Books to return — why didn't Lucy come herself? Because she doesn't want to face you just now, of course, which means exactly what you think it means. . . .

Steven was standing and smiling down at her. His face had lost its preoccupation; he looked tired and a little shy again. "Better go on back yourself before you catch pneumonia. I don't want Oliver on my neck for —"

"You've got him," said Oliver in the door-way. "Getting the place in shape, Elizabeth?"

His voice was easy and unsurprised; for an instant his eyes were not. Silently, her head high, Elizabeth led the way down the hill.

If the house had been empty before it was suddenly overflowing. Maire and Jeep, over-excited by their first long day in the snow, were exchanging tears of fury; Noreen, her face distressed, was wheedling and putting away snowsuits and setting eggs to boil all at once. Constance, unwrapping groceries in the kitchen, began a measured denunciation of the butcher. Steven, who had walked, was persuaded to have a drink while he called Lucy to drive over for him.

Elizabeth remembered later the tiny oasis of peace when Oliver drew her forcibly into the dining-room and nodded at a silver pitcher on the buffet. "Roses," he said shortly.

And roses they were, a warm, just-unfurling dozen of them jammed uncompromisingly into the pitcher. On second thought Oliver had apparently given them a rearranging pull; there was one standing on its head on cherrywood. Roses, and an early arrival home — good omen, or bad? Elizabeth didn't care just then. The sight of Oliver's face, so like

Jeep's when he had tried to help and ruined everything — half-defiant, half-sad — made her throat go rigid. She said sedately, "Thank you," and met Oliver's eyes. "You should see what happened to the last man who brought me roses."

"I know, terrible things," said Oliver in a different voice. "Go comb your hair, it's full of snow."

She didn't immediately go. She crossed to the roses and touched a satin petal and listened, and was lulled by what she heard. Oliver coming back to the doorway, his eyebrows up, saying, "Old-fashioned? The mice have been at the gin again." Constance commenting on the vagaries of the oven. Noreen saying pleadingly, "Oh, Maire, darling, don't — you're much too nice a girl to —" And a crash, proving that Maire was not. Bellows from Jeep. Steven's voice, surmounting Jeep's with an effort: "That sounds like our car."

It was all noisy, normal, safe . . . wasn't it?

This is nonsense, Elizabeth thought lucidly, I'll look back at it and wonder how I could ever have been such an idiot . . . *damn!* Her fingers had moved too suddenly among the roses, and a trio of petals went flaring soundlessly down.

And later she did look back, and knew that she would never come closer to a lightning glimpse into someone else's brain.

Later, too, she clocked herself with lipstick and powderpuff and comb, and knew that not quite seven minutes elapsed between the time she went upstairs and the moment when she reached the lower hall again and that odd awkward hush.

Into it Lucy Brent said, "Oh, what a shame —" and Constance, "It's a wonder the whole thing didn't go." Oliver, sounding like a stranger, said grimly, "I'll take it," and Noreen answered distantly, "Oh, no, Mr. March, I have everything right here."

Elizabeth walked through the living-room without glancing at any of them. She stopped short at the entrance to the dining-room — seeing, for a foolish second not believing, the vivid storm of petals that turned the floor red, the headless rose stems, formal and frightening, still arching serenely in the silver pitcher.

# 3

"Look," said Oliver wearily at six o'clock. "It's too bad, but it's not like losing a leg. The kids —"

"They wouldn't do that. Jeep couldn't reach, to begin with, and Maire wouldn't."

"All right — would Lucy or Steven? Or Constance or I? Would you?"

I didn't, thought Elizabeth desperately. Three petals, that was all; I counted them. If I'm not sure of that, then I'm not sure of anything. I did go right upstairs after that, I did . . . didn't I?

Oliver left his chair and walked restlessly to a window; his voice came muffledly over his shoulder. "Mysteries We Never Solved, No. 2000. What does it matter anyway?"

"I think," said Elizabeth stonily, "that it matters a great deal when someone pulls the heads off a dozen roses or a dozen anything. If you think about it, it's quite an odd thing to do."

Into the silence after that Constance said vaguely and hopefully, "Accidents . . ." and it was as though she hadn't spoken at all.

Oliver swung around and gave Elizabeth a long direct look. "All right," he said abruptly, "let's get it straight, then, if it bothers you. Let's have Maire again, shall we?"

Elizabeth bitterly resented the scene that followed. Maire, who had already denied anything to do with the roses, denying it more vehemently. Oliver saying patiently, "It's all right, honey, no one's going to scold you. We just want to know, and then we'll all forget it. I bet it was fun — was it?" and Maire, her face already a bewildered scarlet, bursting into frightened sobs because her three-year-old world had turned upside down and she didn't know how to defend herself.

Elizabeth cried at last, "Oh, stop it, can't you see she's telling the truth?"

Noreen, silently disapproving, had gone upstairs to put Jeep into his bath. Oliver kissed Maire, perched her on his shoulder and carried her up. Constance said in a low voice, "You know, of course, what it must have been. Noreen had some sort of accident with them, and then did that to make it look like the children. She seemed quite upset when she was cleaning up."

Elizabeth shook her head. "You didn't talk to her."

In the kitchen, shaking the crimson flutter

37

into the wastebasket, Noreen had glanced up apologetically. "I'm so sorry, Mrs. March. I tried to get it all cleaned up before anyone saw."

Elizabeth had a flicker of hope. "Oh, I see. You —"

The girl coloured instantly, her eyes wide and startled. "Oh, I didn't, Mrs. March. Your lovely flowers — I can't imagine how it happened. . . ."

No way out there, because her bewilderment was like Maire's and there was, although for different reasons, the same inability to fight back. And because Elizabeth was almost sure she had caught in Noreen's eyes, and had had to pretend to overlook, the same incredulous speculation she had caught in Oliver's.

Dinner, coffee; Constance and Oliver a little more talkative than usual and sending — weren't they? — worried messages at each other. Elizabeth found herself always one topic behind, felt her mouth curving meaninglessly and her gaze too absorbed, as though she were the hostess and these two difficult guests. There was still the evening to get through, three hours of it if she were to cling to normalcy, to behave as though nothing had happened at all.

As though adult hands hadn't deliberately

38

torn and mutilated the roses. Not an accident, with the stripped stems standing formally in the pitcher, but the mockery of mischief, a frightful parody of a prank. As though evil had gone romping through the house.

The book on the Hiss trial; where had she left off? Elizabeth went through the motions of finding her place and glanced up instead at the quiet room around her.

At the desk at the other end of the room, Constance was seated solidly at her evening pastime of recipe-clipping. Lamplight shone down on the pale brown hair, profiled the long nose, the musing lips, the faintly stubborn chin. It was, thought Elizabeth, like a character-cameo: the odd mixture of greed and austerity, naïveté and a disapproving fortyish firmness. While she watched, her cousin held up a clipping and frowned at it, and the scissors flashed with a surprising violence, slivering the paper.

Oliver, stretched at an easy angle in the deep leather chair, was intent on a newspaper column, dark head bent. She couldn't see his eyes, but his mouth looked sceptical. His whole attitude was completely absorbed in what he was reading. She had been mistaken at dinner, then; he had forgotten about the roses, he —

Without warning, Oliver's eyes met hers over the edge of newspaper. There was nothing casual about the suddenly lifted glance. He was doing, Elizabeth thought, exactly what she was doing — pretending to read, wondering, remembering. She dropped her own gaze sedulously, turned a page.

Two alternatives: which was nicer?

She hadn't left the dining-room when she thought she had; she had simply stood there, her fingers following an independent pattern of their own, her mind not registering this.

Or someone else had come by and wrenched the heads off the roses. If she lifted the protective covering off the 'someone else' it became Steven or Lucy Brent, or Constance or Oliver. There was also the possibility that Noreen was lying, but if that were true then Maire could be lying too, and Maire was not.

Steven, Lucy, Constance — Oliver.

Could this, wondered Elizabeth raggedly, be what we are going to do about Elizabeth?

Eleven o'clock was the normal time of release. Elizabeth rose and was startled to find how easily deception came. The yawn, the casual "I'll look at the children, shall I?" to Oliver, the carrying out of the coffee cups. In the upper hall Constance said abruptly, "You look terribly tired, Elizabeth. Why don't you

40

stay in bed tomorrow — just read and nap? Noreen's here and there won't be anything I can't take care of."

"I might," Elizabeth said, and forced a smile. "You're awfully good, Constance. I don't know what I'd have done without you."

"Nonsense." Constance blushed through her briskness. "It's been nice for me too, you know. Hadn't you better take one of your pills tonight . . . ?"

'It's been nice'; did that mean Constance was about to conclude her visit? Elizabeth went along the hall to the children's room and opened the door with caution. All she could see of Maire under the quilt was pink-gold curls and an outflung arm; she nearly stepped on Jeep, peacefully asleep on the floor beside his crib. She stooped, lifted him into the crib, kissed the warm cheek gently and pulled up the covers. Jeep made an instant and drowsy demand for his truck. She found it, put it into the groping fingers and tiptoed out.

There was no hope of pretending sleep before Oliver tonight; he was there in the bedroom when she came in. Elizabeth turned down her bed and got undressed in silence. Oliver took studs out of his shirt cuffs, put them in a leather box and said casually, "By the way, when do you go to Hathaway?"

"For my checkup? The first week in December — I've got it down somewhere. Why?"

"You don't" — Oliver whipped off his tie — "think you ought to go sooner?"

"What for?" Deception was effortless just so far, and besides, she had to know whether there was substance to the shadow in Oliver's eyes. She said very slowly, "Hathaway's only an obstetrician, you know."

Silence. Oliver moved roughly away from the bureau and took a cigarette from his bedside table without looking. He said coolly, "And what's the inner meaning of that?"

"This." Why was it so like taking a hurdle? "As you've pointed out, the affair of the roses was no tragedy. But it happened. Weirdly enough, it seems to me that you've a notion I did it."

There never used to be these blanks, she thought, these moments when we both go off away from each other and all the lines of communication are down. What's happened, what's making us behave this way?

Oliver seemed to have had the same wonder; he swung to face her. "Elizabeth —"

She would not be melted, she would not be forced into remembering the way things had been. She said evenly, "You do think so, Oliver, don't you?"

The match he had been holding flickered

out. He said without lighting another, with halts between the words, "You were — thinking about something else. My God, everybody pulls up grass and plucks at wicker and peels off bark — it's the nature of the beast. What the hell," said Oliver, suddenly and explosively violent, "does it matter, and why do we have to keep on talking about it? I'm sorry I ever brought the damned things home."

"That," observed Elizabeth stiffly into the sudden darkness, "was prettily put."

"I suppose it was. Sorry. Maybe it was a cunning florist's trick . . . let's forget it anyway. End of episode."

His voice sounded sleepy. Elizabeth lay rigid, her mind slipping back to yesterday and that disturbing sense of unease, like the slyest of motions somewhere in the background.

She hadn't caught the motion itself, or the hand. But this, the roses, was the very tangible proof of its existence. This, and not Oliver and Lucy — or perhaps an off-shoot of Oliver and Lucy — was what had made her afraid.

Afraid, under the softest possible blankets, with her husband not six feet away and her children safely, healthily asleep only a wall's thickness from her. More afraid than she had ever been in her life, because there was nothing to fight.

Bells counted themselves distantly in the clear cold night. Five of us, all told, thought Elizabeth, turning restlessly on her other side. Five and maybe one more, whom all of us know and one of us won't admit, something that isn't flesh and bone but more of an entity than any of us. . . . Finally, interruptedly, she slept.

Thanksgiving came and went; in the face of Constance's mute horror Elizabeth sewed up the turkey with red thread and felt ridiculously gay. It was impossible not to with the children in the kitchen; they formed an instant and devoted attachment to the docile creature in the roasting pan. Jeep said dubiously, "Might bite you," and Maire said earnestly, "No, he *loves* you, Jeep," and the turkey went into the oven amid pattings and farewells.

And even after that there were days when everything was almost all right. Almost, because it was as though there were a wall of glass between herself and Oliver. They could speak and smile through it, and go briskly about their lives on either side of it, but it was there. Elizabeth forgot that at times until she bumped into it and hurt herself.

There were the other days, when the children caught her mood and translated it in their own disastrous fashion. Maire had perfected her technique and could now not only cry like a baby but like a whole nursery full of babies; the sound of it sawed ceaselessly at Elizabeth's nerves. Jeep was like a small rogue elephant: the phonograph suddenly stopped functioning, toys fell magically to pieces, the breakage in the kitchen shot up at an appalling rate.

Elizabeth, clinging grimly to calm, thought, Careful, this is like virus. Nothing to do but wait it out.

Oddly enough, in spite of the betraying words that kept echoing in her brain, she found Lucy Brent a welcome distraction. Lucy was a being from another world, crisp, definite, untroubledly sure of herself. If the other woman noticed a subtle change in their relationship — and very little escaped the brilliant dark eyes behind the restless flow of chatter — she said nothing.

Lucy was there on the third of December, when Elizabeth's bank statement came. She said, "Aren't you lucky! All I ever get around the first of the month is bills," and stood. "Steven's home, feeling frightful, and I really should be there to stroke his brow. Mind if I phone the drug store first?"

"Go ahead," Elizabeth said absently. It was a barren mail — soap coupons, what looked like an advertisement addressed to Oliver, the bank statement. At the phone, Lucy asked for the pharmacist. Elizabeth slit the long brown envelope, looked at her balance, which was surprisingly less than she'd thought, and ruffled idly through the cancelled cheques. Constance, cash, the stocking shop, Noreen, Noreen, Noreen, cash again . . . and what was this?

In her first casual glance Elizabeth thought it was a cheque she'd written while she was still in the hospital; her signature looked somehow laborious, not quite her own. She pulled the cheque free of the others and examined it, and Lucy's voice and the room around her dropped away in her sudden incredulous attention to the slip of pale blue in her hand.

The cheque was made out to Sarah E. Bennett, Noreen's predecessor, in the amount of her week's salary, thirty-five dollars. It was dated October 29th, and everything was in order except that that was nearly two weeks after Mrs. Bennett had departed for Canada to take over the household of a suddenly widowed sister, and the handwriting was not Elizabeth's.

Altogether, there were three of them.

# 4

"What's the matter?" asked Lucy amusedly. "Overdrawn?"

"What? . . . No, not this time." Elizabeth went to the door with Lucy, as conscious and careful of the cheques in her hand as though she were holding a loaded gun. "I hope Steven's better. Give him our best, will you?"

Constance was moving briskly about in the upper hall; from the children's room came intermittent thumps and shouts of delight. She was safe, for a few minutes at least; she could examine the forgeries more closely.

Someone had been very careful over these. It had taken time and practice even to approximate the intricate loops and angles of Elizabeth's handwriting. She went to the desk and got out a cancelled cheque, cashed in September, and compared it with the forgeries — and yes, the 'Sarah E. Bennett' was particularly good, even to the scrambling backtrack with which the t's were crossed. The writer had evidently been more nervous over Elizabeth's signature; it had a cautious look. But, she found, it had improved. The first was palpably odd to anyone who knew her writing well; the third would easily have fooled, for instance, Oliver.

"Elizabeth?" said Constance inquiringly at the head of the stairs.

She put the cheques back in the envelope and went up in a dream. Constance, dismayingly real and severe, confronted her at the linen closet. "Elizabeth, I do think something should be done about the laundry. Just look at this — they've sent you another sheet that doesn't belong to you."

She held out the offending linen, and Elizabeth gave it an uncaring glance. "Oh. Is it in reasonably good condition, do you suppose?"

"I haven't looked," said Constance affrontedly. "Here — just feel it for yourself. It's obviously a Coarse Percale."

Who else could have made an epithet out of that? wondered Elizabeth giddily. 'I don't care what you say about him, he's nothing but a Coarse Percale.' Aloud she said guiltily, "I suppose I ought to speak to them. If you'd put it up on the top shelf —"

". . . You'll forget all about it," finished Constance, smiling faintly. "If you don't mind my doing it, I'll just take care of it myself."

Elizabeth must have replied to that, because in another instant she was in her own bedroom, the door closed, the perfidious sheet sponged out of her mind then and forever. She was aware, as she sat down on her bed, of the slow shocked pounding of her heart. She singled out the three cheques again and turned them over. One hundred and five dollars — but still considerate of whoever had written them, because wasn't she liable?

The endorsement on the backs was small and wooden, totally unlike Mrs. Bennett's flourishing hand. No worry for the forger there, because Mrs. Bennett had cashed her cheques locally and these had been cashed at Elizabeth's bank. Nos. 351, 353, and 354. The attempt on No. 352 had apparently failed to measure up.

Not Mrs. Bennett — not even if she were still in the country and Elizabeth had surprised her with cheques and tracing-paper and pen; not Mrs. Bennett whose final parting had been accomplished with an unashamed sniffle.

But someone who had access to Elizabeth's personalized cheques, kept in the desk in the living-room. Someone who had the opportunity to remove and study a cancelled cheque for the proper amount and the manner of writing Sarah Bennett's name.

A woman, posing briefly and boldly as Sarah Bennett.

Mr. Delbow, assistant cashier, said briskly, "Now, if you'll just sign this stop-payment order — it's required, you understand. We'll send you affidavits in the course of a day or two, and if you'll sign and return those . . ."

He was more than a little puzzled about Mrs. Oliver March, head bent as she wrote her name on a form at the corner of his desk, stone martens looped about the expensively tailored shoulders of her suit. His reassurances that she hadn't lost on the forged cheques — "When we pay out money over a faulty signature the liability is ours, Mrs. March" — hadn't brought the colour back into the noticeably pale pointed face. And it was very hard to read the eyes behind the brief black veiling.

He had already exhausted the possibilities of Mrs. Bennett; he had summoned the teller who had handled the cheque cashed at this, the main branch. All three cheques had been cashed within the course of two hours, the latter two at a branch in the West End. The tellers concerned had written Mrs. Bennett's address on the backs of the cheques; in no case had the identification presented been noted down, which was in itself a rule of the bank.

Mr. Delbow said as Elizabeth restored his pen, "This means, of course, Mrs. March, that whoever wrote these cheques has some identification belonging to Mrs. Bennett. Otherwise the cheques wouldn't have been cashed at all."

She merely nodded. The assistant cashier then explained that although the bank would attempt prosecution the chances of their finding the culprit were almost negligible unless the forger should turn out to be an habitual offender. To his bewilderment, he could have sworn that Mrs. March looked relieved. He said, "I'll have the amount credited to your account at once," and she stood up, gathering her gloves and bag, giving him a sudden wry smile.

"The odd part of all this is that I've been banking here nearly four years and when *I* try to cash a cheque your people stop just short of fingerprinting."

"Always the way," murmured Mr. Delbow musically, putting a guiding hand on her arm; "always the way, isn't it?"

The interview at the bank had taken longer

than she expected; Elizabeth, driving toward home, got caught in early commuter traffic and sat through a succession of red lights with an anxious eye on her watch. It was very important to get home before Oliver if her trip to Boston were to look purely casual — and she had been instantly determined that Oliver, to whom she would once have turned instinctively, should know nothing at all about the forgeries.

Because Oliver, mercilessly logical, would disregard personalities when he arrived at a list of the only possible suspects. Such a frighteningly short list, when the name of your own cousin was on it. It was, of course, unthinkable that Constance . . . But would Oliver recognize that?

Elizabeth sounded her horn curtly, passed a Cadillac proceeding at a waddle, and was clear of the traffic. At a little after five o'clock it was almost dark; only a dimming lip of icy lemon light on the horizon separated the marshes from the sky. The evening was bleak, windy. With the car heater turned on full, Elizabeth was cold to the core.

October 29th the cheques had been cashed, the first at 10.14 A.M., the second at 12.46 P.M. On October 29th she had been home from the hospital only three days, and the whole of that interval was a clouded dream, distant, unreal, further blurred by the sedatives she took when the before-dawn dark became intolerable. She had been aware of the household functioning dimly below her, but apart from Constance's brisk consultations and Noreen's occasional worried entrance, it might have been the household of another woman.

How, then, to pin it down to a presence here, an undeniable absence there? It wasn't so simple a matter as Noreen, Lucy, Constance, because Mr. Delbow had picked up instantly a detail that she had missed. Two pens had been used in the forging of the cheques, which suggested the possibility of a companion. "Probably," the assistant cashier had said thoughtfully, "a man. It generally is in cases of this type."

Elizabeth watched her headlights streaming into the dark. She said to herself firmly, You don't know what associates Mrs. Bennett had, or how often they came to the house when we were out. How simple for one of them to take the necessary materials, to —

If she had been speaking aloud, it would have stuck in her throat; as it was her mind stopped dead, mocking her. It pointed out that the cheques, like the roses, like the subtle malaise pervading her home, were the result of evil ripening and swelling and finally beginning to seep out behind a known and trusted face.

Elizabeth put an involuntary hand to her temple, pressing upwards; brought it back to the wheel. No time for desperation when you were driving, no time for an uprush of fear.

She was home before Oliver, but just barely; by the time she had changed her suit and come downstairs again, Oliver was in the kitchen and the children had forgotten their supper in the usual torrent of delight. Noreen was standing by in smiling resignation. At Elizabeth's entrance Oliver turned a look of unconvincing severity on the children, who were jumping and clambering at his overcoat pockets. "*After* your supper. Hello, hon."

His kiss grazed Elizabeth's cheekbone. She said lightly, "Hello — aren't you cold!" and moved easily away. "Maire, *not* your fingers. . . ."

Maire ate scrambled eggs out of her palm, swung her legs in excitement and said in her high clear voice, "Daddy, Mama was in Boston!" Jeep echoed her, not quite as comprehensibly, and they both turned a look of admiration on Elizabeth, who busied herself instantly at the toaster. She had forgotten that to the children Boston was a magical end-of-the-world place, for the simple reason that

Oliver went there every morning.

At her side Noreen murmured, "I don't think it's quite done," and Oliver, hanging up his overcoat, said, "Did you really go into town, or is this from the usually unreliable source?"

She hadn't meant to lie to Oliver, she hadn't meant the matter to come up at all. But this, her first trip into Boston since the hospital . . . and Oliver's eyes were not as casual as his voice. She told him what she had told Constance: "You know those books I ordered from Haysmith's — I thought they might have come in and he'd forgotten all about me."

"Why, the old fool," said Oliver, mildly amazed. "I happened to be near there just before I came home, and thought I'd check. He could at least have told me you'd been in."

Had he gone to Haysmith's, or was this a test? Elizabeth thought bitterly, Just because you're lying doesn't mean he is, and said, "The shop was quite busy, I suppose he forgot."

Outwardly, that was the end of it; to Elizabeth, who carried the deception about with her like a stone all that evening, it had the frightening aspect of a beginning. This was how people put distance between each other, and couldn't close it again because there were too many lies, too many subterfuges to cross with any kind of dignity. Most marriages didn't, as people said, go on the rocks, because that implied a sudden and smashing impact. It wasn't that, it was a slow day-by-day inching away from closeness, so that eventually another goal was nearer than your marriage and it was easier to go forward than to go back.

Is this, thought Elizabeth huntedly, what we are doing to each other — and to the children, who should matter more than either of us?

She knocked at Constance's door before she went to bed, aware, and disliking it, that she was looking for a way to cross the most shocking name off that short ugly list. There couldn't be any questions, but you could find reassurance in a glance, a gesture. . . .

But she didn't. There was a pause before the answering, "Elizabeth? Come in," and then a rapid rustling of taffeta. When Elizabeth opened the door Constance was sitting at her dressing-table, her hair out of its smooth daytime rolls, her long face a little flushed. Her eyes under their thick white lids were fleetingly the eyes of a stranger, quick, sharp, measuring. If she had opened the door without knocking, Elizabeth wondered shakenly, would there have been quite another scene, quite another Constance?

That was ridiculous, and — frightening. Constance had been getting ready for bed, of course, and had tried on the taffeta housecoat Elizabeth had given her for her birthday weeks ago; that would account for the swift crisp motion of fabric that had followed her knock.

Constance's gaze became suddenly inquiring; Elizabeth, searching vacantly for a pretext, seized on the housecoat. "I was right, that's a marvellous colour for you. Does it fit?"

"Oh yes. That is, I think —" Constance was nervous. She stood too suddenly and one balancing hand sent something crashing lightly to the surface of the dressing-table. Elizabeth glanced idly down; it was a photograph of herself, the one her publishers had used for the back of her first book jacket. She was looking slantingly down and across the camera. Her hair had been longer then, and a delicate angling of light emphasized the pale backward lift of it. The photograph hadn't been in the guest room when Constance came, thought Elizabeth idly, it hadn't been there —

Constance was waiting; she forced herself back to attentiveness and an admiring inspection of the housecoat. She wished, as she said

57

good night and went along the hall, that she had never knocked at her cousin's door, that she hadn't seen her photograph there. That she hadn't heard that hurrying rustle, as though taffeta arms had gone up hastily to re-arrange lifted-back hair.

# 5

December was snowy, and made of elastic. Elizabeth got through the days with a determined briskness, plunging into her Christmas shopping, which she dreaded ordinarily, with a fervour that astonished everyone around her. Maire talked about sleds; Jeep, for reasons known only to himself, hoped ardently for a fly-swatter.

There were a number of things to remember the early part of December by, and Elizabeth remembered them all; while October 29th had dropped into a void and was just now sending up echoes, every day had become a new day of battle. And battle with what? Shadows, nerves, imagination . . . ?

No. Forged cheques were made of paper and ink, and cunning.

Maire plummeted the full length of the stairs on her head and had to be rushed to the hospital for X-rays. Jeep stuffed his panda into the toilet, flushed it, and consulted nobody about the mounting level of water on the bathroom floor; when he had tired of watching it he simply went away. The kitchen ceiling dried eventually, and Oliver, looking like a man determined to hold his tongue at all costs, painted it laboriously.

Hathaway's nurse called up and postponed Elizabeth's appointment; she reported this stiffly and conscientiously to Oliver, who met her eyes and glanced quickly away. Gradually, and somewhere in herself terrified that it could happen at all, she accustomed herself to two existences that overlapped but never blended.

There was the one in which everything was what it seemed, and she was a dutiful mother to the children and the reasonable facsimile of a wife to Oliver, and went about with Lucy Brent and succumbed to Steven's quiet encouragement sufficiently to spend grim, trying-to-work hours up in the studio.

There was the other one, in which she was alone and afraid, cut off from appeal by the dread of further damaging her marriage. In which, if she let her desperately fixed attention flicker, everything might topple, and anything might happen.

Like the roses, like the misty date of October 29th when a woman pretending to be Sarah Bennett had walked into Elizabeth's bank, it was nothing you could put an accusing finger on. It was like a picture delicately out of drawing, or a phonograph record with a slightly warped centre. It was all wrong only if you knew and loved the view or the melody.

But it was calculated; there was a brain behind it, wholly concerned with the quiet growth of fear.

It was, perhaps most of all, the affair of Jeep's birthday on the thirteenth of December.

There was protocol on Jeep's birthday. Ten minutes after Oliver had had his first glimpse of his son, while Elizabeth was still pleasantly giddy over a long-awaited cigarette, they had agreed never to lose Jeep in the Christmas rush. "Who knows, it might warp him for life," Oliver had said, "so as long as the funds hold out, let's keep him separate. Did you know you were burning a hole in your bedspread, Mrs. March?"

So there was as much panoply over Jeep's birthday as though it had fallen in July. Presents, and something in the way of consolation for Maire, all to be opened when Oliver arrived with ice cream and candles for the cake. Everything was wrapped and waiting at five-thirty, and the children, who had been asking since morning, "Is it Jeep's birthday yet?" had obligingly disappeared. For no reason at all

61

Elizabeth was startled when the fall of the knocker turned out to be Steven Brent.

He was diffident, standing against the icy dark, sensing her surprise at once and half turning away. The porch lamp made his hair very fair, deepened the lines in the shy tired face. "Crale saw the synopsis today and likes it very much. There are just a couple of things . . . but you're busy, so I'll —"

"Not at all, come on in."

Elizabeth took him out to the sunporch where they wouldn't be disturbed and switched on lamps. Light flowed softly over the rope rug, woven in golden parquet squares, over yellow and red armchairs, a fat black hassock, a wall of windows glimmeringly full of reflections. They sat on the couch at the end of the long narrow room; Steven put the typed synopsis and its manila envelope on the coffee table and frowned absently at a memo in his hand.

"As I say, Crale's most enthusiastic. He does question, and I must admit that I do, too, the fact that the daughter who wilfully vanishes doesn't make more of an effort to communicate with the mother. Don't you think . . ."

It was a plot Elizabeth had been playing with for two years; she knew every twist and turn and objection and she could let her attention wander. She came in nicely at intervals with, "Oh, not necessarily, don't forget she's fortyish," or, "You're quite right, I hadn't thought of that." In between, she found herself studying the man beside her on the couch.

Of them all, Steven hadn't changed. He was still shy, quiet, concerned — vividly aware of nuances, comfortably silent about them. You forgot your tenseness with Steven because of his very receptiveness. Elizabeth was totally unprepared when he let the memo flutter to the coffee table and took off his glasses with a driven air and said, "Look here, Elizabeth, let's do this some other time. You've probably gathered that this isn't what I came about at all."

Somewhere in the middle of that, Oliver was standing in the open doorway, and in the near distance Noreen's voice said hurriedly, "Oh, I think Mrs. March is —" and then died.

It was almost, thought Elizabeth, as though the girl had tried to thrust herself bodily between Oliver and the porch door. Surely Noreen wasn't mad enough to think —

She hadn't time for that because Oliver, packages in his arms, was smiling at her inquiringly and Steven was standing, bundling the synopsis back into its envelope. "I'm just on my way — I've been trying to get your wife back to the grindstone."

"Where she belongs," said Oliver mildly. His eyes weren't mild. Bluer than Maire's, bluer even than Jeep's, they rested briefly on Elizabeth and it was almost like a quick angry touch of his hand. His gaze flicked to Steven, he said politely, "Time for a drink?" But it was only that, the barest politeness.

Steven was aware of it; his glance at Oliver was quiet. "Can't, thanks, I've been too late as it is. I'll leave this with you, Elizabeth, and give you a ring in a day or so. . . ."

He was gone and there was a moment at the door when Elizabeth felt as though she, too, should be saying good night to the overcoated stranger beside her. Then the door closed, and Oliver was again her husband, a man she loved through a glass wall; and Oliver was saying, "Are you really back at work? Good. . . . Let's have the birthday and then a drink. Where are the kids?"

They usually flew to the door; with instinctive perversity they hadn't tonight. "Up in their room, I guess. I'll get them," Elizabeth said, and escaped up the stairs from Oliver's brilliant scrutiny. If there was to be this, an awkwardness every time she discussed her book with her editor —

Maire was sitting on her bed, ruffling through a book of animal photographs; Jeep, chanting tonelessly, was involved with plastic scissors and a magazine on the floor. He had a dull and thwarted look because the scissors wouldn't cut, none of his usual loud fury. Noreen, folding laundry into the bureau drawers, looked up and smiled with an air of held-in excitement. Elizabeth said brightly, "Daddy's home, and it's Jeep's birthday. Happy birthday, Jeep. Aren't you going to come down and see what you've got besides cake and ice cream?"

They came, lethargically. Noreen, smiling and scolding anxiously, hurried down the stairs to set the table in the dining-room. Elizabeth, wondering, watched Jeep unwrap his presents — a fleet of tiny trucks, a dog whose tongue lapped in and out when you pulled him, a miniature merry-go-round. There was no spark anywhere; it was as though Jeep had been waked up in the middle of the night and brought down to admire his toys, puzzled, sleepy, half resentful.

Elizabeth glanced alertly at Maire and saw the same thing. She had scoured the town for a pig of suitable size and expression, and had found at last a calico animal with lifelike white lashes and a foolish smile tucked under its snout. Maire opened it and said with a glimmer of animation, "Pig," and then put it carelessly down on the floor. Noreen said softly,

"Oh, darling, what a beautiful pig." Her eyes met Elizabeth's apprehensively.

Oliver said, "Looks like we've come to the wrong party. Maybe the ice cream . . . ?"

Constance had come down; she said sedately, "Happy birthday, Jeep," and presented a rubber fire truck. Noreen brought in the cake and lighted the candles and put ice cream in two dishes. Oliver watched the children mounting the unaccustomed chairs and said suddenly, "Know something? They're sick."

"Nonsense," said Elizabeth, firm but worried. "What have they had today, Noreen?"

"Just their lunch, Mrs. March, and a light one — bacon and string beans and custard — because I knew they'd be having their birthday supper. But they do look —"

It wasn't long in the deciding. Maire fiddled with her spoon; Jeep, gluttonous, swallowed two fat mouthfuls and returned them with a surprised air to the rug. Noreen sprang for cloths, Constance said thoughtfully, "Well, you know, they didn't seem quite —" and Oliver transported Jeep to the bathroom.

Elizabeth, oddly frightened, said, "Maire, you've been eating something, both of you. What was it?"

And Maire, pale and docile, said, "Candy."

"Show me." Elizabeth was crisp and com-

66

manding, not letting the panic show. It was a mark of how dreadfully familiar she was growing with her enemy, the subtle creator of her other world, that she never for an instant doubted the source of the candy.

But this was the first time it had touched the children.

There had evidently been a great deal of candy — bon-bons, from the look of the crumpled foils, purple and green and silver, stuffed in a greedy shining heap into the bottom of the children's toy chest. Not the kind of candy you gave wholesale to children, unless you wanted to bring about exactly what had happened. Elizabeth looked hard at Maire and gradually her legs stopped trembling; the child's eyes were heavy and a little glazed and she had one hand pressed exploringly to her stomach, but — she could say it now, she could face it in her own mind — the candy hadn't been poisoned.

The door opened and Oliver thrust Jeep into the room. "He's empty," he said briefly, and met Elizabeth's eyes. "I'll leave this to you, shall I?"

Elizabeth turned down Maire's bed, lifted Jeep into his crib, and began some casual, off-hand questions. She realized almost at once that it was useless, because the children didn't know where the candy had come from. They had found it there in their toy chest, and it was only sensible to eat it as fast and as furtively as possible because otherwise it would have been taken away from them.

"But there must have been a box." Elizabeth met Maire's eyes and said with firmness, "Candy *always* comes in a box. Or a bag."

She waited. Jeep said ponderingly, "Where box, Mama?" and Maire thought it over and went to investigate the toy chest. She said very positively, "It was just in there, just like that."

Just like that — spilled carelessly there, glittering and gay to catch a child's eye at the time of day when they picked up their toys with reluctance and returned them helter-skelter to the chest. Elizabeth was carefully bright. "Then someone must have come into your room and left them there for a surprise. Who could *that* have been?"

"Daddy," said Jeep promptly.

"No, not Daddy. Who else has —"

"Maire," said Jeep with an air of fond finality.

"No. Maire, who else has been —"

The door opened and Noreen came in, her face clearing at the sight of the children sitting alertly up in their beds. "Are they all right, Mrs. March? Do you think they're coming down with something?"

"A light attack of bon-bons," Elizabeth

said, rising. Because the children were watching and listening she kept her voice friendly as she said, lifting the foils out of the chest, "Ever seen these around before?"

She didn't hear the first part of Noreen's reply. Staring down at the papers in her own cupped palms, she was suddenly aware that she herself had seen them, or something very like them, not long ago . . . where? When?

". . . some kind of chocolates," Noreen was saying with a worried air. "And they look — expensive, don't they? The children must have found them while I was hanging the laundry — I left them here with their books and told them to start picking up their toys. But where did they come from?"

"That," said Elizabeth lightly, "is the mystery." She kissed the children and went to the doorway. "They're overdue for bed as it is, so let's talk about it later . . ."

But it was Oliver she talked to first. Constance was starting dinner, and Oliver stood motionless at a window in the living-room, staring out into the dark. His back looked grim. At Elizabeth's entrance he said without turning, "They'd done their birthdaying ahead of time, I gather. What was it, did you find out?"

"These." Elizabeth showed him the crumpled foils. "I've a feeling I've seen this brand somewhere before — have you?"

Oliver gave them a short glance. "No. Where in the name of God did they get them?"

Inside Elizabeth a brief astonishment turned to anger. She said evenly, "We'll probably figure it out a little sooner if you don't swear at me," and tossed the papers into the fireplace.

"Yes. Sorry," said Oliver, his tone matching her own. "It isn't serious, he doesn't know what a birthday's all about anyway. But — there's this. Nobody knows where the stuff came from, nobody saw them eat it. Do you, for instance, know what they're doing even half the time — does anybody?"

"If you mean, is somebody at their side every waking instant, no, certainly not," said Elizabeth, stung. "It might be done with one child, if you didn't mind turning out a little marionette, but it can't be done with two."

"I thought that was what Noreen was here for."

"Noreen's very good and very capable, and when the children aren't with her they're with me. Neither of us is a police matron, however, and there are things to be done in the house. She was hanging up the laundry, I gather, when —"

70

"Of course, that's right — you were busy with Steven Brent."

A small shocked silence fell. Somewhere beyond it Constance closed the oven door with a bang, and Noreen tiptoed in the upper hall. Elizabeth and Oliver stood staring at each other, heads flung back, anger like a tightwire strung between them. A moment passed that way before Elizabeth said slowly, "Oliver," and stopped and then started again. "Sooner or later, we've got to —"

Noreen came down the stairs and paused in the doorway. About to speak, she glanced uncertainly at Elizabeth and then at Oliver, and turned and went silently into the kitchen. Constance appeared in the dining-room, brisk and aproned. "What a pity about the children — but they'll have their cake tomorrow."

Nobody answered her. Sleet touched the windows. Oliver opened his newspaper, rattling it, and observed savagely into the folds, "What a rotten night."

"Vile," said Elizabeth stonily.

How long had it been since she went to bed and to sleep, as simply as that? The process was very involved now; it meant the uncomfortable aloneness with Oliver, the polite query as to whether the other intended to read, the attempt at oblivion. After that, the cigarette, the staring thoughts, the sleeping pill which had lately grown into two.

Elizabeth lay in the dark and listened to Oliver sleeping. The vague dread that she had first become aware of a month ago was taking a more definite shape. It was now a pair of hands. Tearing the roses, as though they hadn't been able to resist the beauty and the perfection, or the gesture they represented. Patiently practicing with a pen — how many sheets of paper, in what quiet room, had been covered with 'Sarah E. Bennett' and 'Elizabeth March'? Opening over a child's toy chest, to spill out a shining jumble of rich forbidden candies.

Hands she had looked at countless times, and hadn't really seen because they were the hands of someone she trusted.

The trouble with seconal was that somewhere between the second one and morning, she could shrink and dwindle while the hands swelled and grew and played with her life at their own vicious leisure.

But the cheques, thought Elizabeth, grasping at tangibles, unable to live too long with the hands; something will turn up about the cheques, or Mrs. Bennett's stolen identification. . . .

Something did.

# 6

It was a logical thing, a small but necessary link in the misty, twisted chain. It had its own prologue, and Elizabeth half recognized that at the time.

She had gone up to the studio at a few minutes before noon, because lately she didn't like being alone in the house. The children had been picked up for a pre-Christmas party, and Constance had asked for the car. Noreen, whose day off extended from twelve to twelve the following day, had hurried off to catch her bus.

The studio was bitterly cold. Elizabeth turned on both electric heaters, put a fresh sheet of copy paper in her typewriter, lighted a cigarette and sat staring ahead of her.

The morning hadn't been peaceful. That wasn't due as much to Jeep's biting Maire in a transport of rage, or Maire tearing the leg off his battered rubber baby by way of revenge, as it was to Lucy Brent's late-coffee visit.

Lucy had been at her most Lucyish: nervous, irritatingly brisk, critical. "Haven't you lost weight, Elizabeth?"

"A little, maybe." Which was a lie; it was seven pounds in four weeks.

"Are you feeling as well as you should by now — or oughtn't I to ask?"

Nice points, both of them: how well should you feel when an unseen, uncontrollable presence, the presence of evil, had slipped quietly into the heart of your home? And should Lucy — *Lucy* ask? Elizabeth hadn't had to answer that, because upstairs, dimly, there was a fresh burst of tears, and she was able to murmur, "Poor Noreen. She must be holding her breath until she goes off at noon."

"Noreen's quite good, isn't she?"

"Extremely." Elizabeth felt peculiarly defensive this morning under Lucy's sharp roving gaze. When the other woman busied herself noncommittally with a cigarette, she took a moment for appraisal, a long detached look she wouldn't have dreamed of two months before.

Lucy was — thirty-four, thirty-five? Not tall, with a quick-moving, beautifully economical body that just avoided angularity. Small dark head, small clever face with haughty cheekbones and restless eyes. Like a greyhound turned out by Bonwit's, Elizabeth had thought when they first met; she knew now that Lucy refurbished her own slender wardrobe patiently and expertly.

And what did she know of Lucy, beyond her darting gaiety, her passion for bridge, her deftness with a scarf or a medallion or a twist of silk? Nothing. . . . The impromptu realization brought her up short. Lucy was looking at her and saying with faint amusement, "She doesn't like me, you know. I don't think she approves. Noreen, I mean."

"Nonsense," said Elizabeth surprisedly, and when Lucy smiled and shrugged her wonder took on an edge of annoyance. "What a peculiar thing to think. For that matter, you've never liked her, have you, Lucy?"

Lucy's eyebrows went up. She said mildly, "Like her? My dear, I hardly know her. As far as I'm concerned she's an appendage of the children, and them I adore. . . . Put it down," said Lucy vaguely, "as a funny impression." She smiled her sudden warm banishing smile. "As you may have gathered, I'm not fit to talk to today. I have a horrible thing to ask you, so I will now take a running jump and get it over with. . . . Can you lend me fifty dollars until January?"

"Of course," said Elizabeth. It seemed imperative to be as brisk as Lucy, and not to offer more than fifty. "Will a cheque do?"

"A cheque will do wonders," Lucy said

with frank relief, and thanked Elizabeth and folded it into her wallet. Five minutes later she was moving toward the door, and that was when the children came down the stairs, ready for the party, shepherded by Noreen. That was when Lucy turned, and greeted Maire and Jeep, and lifted her eyes and said brightly, "Hello, Noreen, how are you?"

Noreen bent and adjusted Jeep's suspender straps before she straightened and answered politely, "Hello, Mrs. Brent."

Elizabeth watched with a small shock the glance that went between them: Lucy cool and poised and a little challenging, still holding her mechanical smile; Noreen facing her in her rigidly neat uniform of white blouse and dark blue jumper, her gaze level, her composure matching Lucy's.

For a quick instant it echoed almost audibly on the air that they were not nursemaid and visitor or even oblivious strangers, but hostile, well-aware equals.

She had a plot and a typewriter, peace and pencils; at the end of an hour Elizabeth found that she might as well have been supplied with a shoemaker's awl.

The bon-bons — where had she seen those brilliant foils before? If she could pin that down, she would know who it was . . .

. . . who hated her.

Because that, all at once, was the only possible answer. The simplicity of it was appalling: the loathing that must have bred and spread behind a friendly face, the violence that was forcing the venom out drop by drop, that must sooner or later come with a gush. . . .

Elizabeth felt shaken and a little sick; she got up and walked restlessly around the studio, stopping at the front window to stare down at the house. It was graceful, even under the leafless trees: stormy grey shingle, shuttered in white. The window trim needed painting, so did the rose trellises.

Her gaze halted. She stayed sharply still, fingers tightening in her palms. Because there was an answering-back stare from the quiet, supposedly empty house.

Like war at long range . . . why did she think of that? It was a face, pressed whitely against one of the upper windows, tilted a little in its blind stare up at the studio. It moved a trifle; a white hand lifted lazily. It watched, it waited for a shocking and boundless moment, and then a sudden turn of shoulder took it away out of sight.

It was the window of Noreen's room.

It was not Noreen's face.

Careful. This wasn't the time to slip on a

stone, or plunge head-on into a thrusting branch. Elizabeth, running precipitately down the hill toward the house, closed her mind to what she would find there. She would know, and that was enough — and the only way to do it was pell-mell, like this, with action outdistancing thought and fear.

She reached the house and went in through the kitchen, because that was quicker. Warmth met her, and the secretive knowing silence of a just-emptied house. The oil burner started up with a throb, a board creaked somewhere, the refrigerator gave a mechanical mutter and settled back to work. Elizabeth, catching her breath with difficulty, called uncertainly, "Hello?"

And, at the foot of the stairs, "Constance . . . ?"

But she was alone in the house.

The quality of the silence suggested it; the front door, swinging inward a lazy inch while she waited at the foot of the stairs with lifted face, confirmed it. Someone had flashed down these stairs not much over a minute ago, and had not taken time to close the door securely.

Either that or, out of fear and a nearly sleepless night, she had shaped an innocent reflection into a face, and the door had been left that way earlier.

Upstairs, she found her answer. The door of Noreen's room was ajar, and Elizabeth went in. It was a small room, slant-ceilinged, wallpapered in a pattern of ivy and curly pink flowers. There was a single bed and night table, a bureau, an armchair, a hooked rug full of clear pastels.

Throughout the air hung a heavy sweet perfume, alien to Elizabeth, clearly wrong in that room.

There were two glass bottles on the bureau. Elizabeth uncapped them, sniffed at innocuous flower fragrances and replaced them carefully. Outside Constance's door she hesitated a moment and then went in.

Her cousin's usually immaculate room was untidy today; to see the tweed suit Constance had worn that morning flung carelessly on the bed and a rejected stocking draped rakishly over a chair was almost like catching Constance herself with no clothes on. Elizabeth had no real attention for the room. She went to the dressing-table, tested a tall bottle of cologne and found it to be gardenia, and paused. Her heartbeats refused to quiet, the palms of her hands felt damp. What was this sense of urgent hurry, almost of personal danger?

She pulled her thoughts back. Whoever had worn that drench of perfume hadn't applied it here, unless — At the back of the dressing-table, near the mirror, was a small something in pink and white striped wrapping. It had been opened and loosely re-wrapped. Before Elizabeth's scruples could catch up with her fingers the striped paper had fallen away.

It was perfume — imported, costly — in a chaste, unopened white box. There was a card, and on it was written simply, "I hope you will accept this from H. W."

Elizabeth came aware suddenly of Constance's bedside clock. How long since she had come into the house — five minutes, six? She closed the door of her cousin's bedroom behind her and went down the stairs to the telephone. She heard her own voice, expressionless, giving the Brents' number, and then she waited and listened to the patient, empty drawl. She was about to hang up when the receiver at the other end was lifted with a jostling sound and Lucy's voice, breathless, said, "Hello? Yes, hello, who is it?"

Breathless.

"Elizabeth. I wondered if by any chance you still had . . ."

Moments later, after pretending to write down an address she didn't want, Elizabeth put the receiver back. The silent house, the witnessing walls and watchful mirrors that could have told her everything she wanted to know, were full of suggestions.

She didn't listen. She made herself a sandwich and tea, turned on a lamp against the threatening light, and settled down grimly with a book. Before she did any of those things she did a thing she had never done before: nonchalantly, trying not to notice herself doing it, she locked every door in the house.

The thing that turned up so neatly and logically, its purpose spent, was Mrs. Bennett's pocketbook.

Noreen brought it to Elizabeth the next afternoon. "Excuse me, Mrs. March, but would you have any idea whose this is?"

Elizabeth took the bag and looked at it carefully. It was old and worn, its top clasp tarnished, its black fabric folds dusty. Mrs. Bennett's cheerful voice seemed to emanate from it: "Oh, don't trouble your head about it, Mrs. March, it'll turn up, and small loss if it doesn't. It was an old thing anyway — nothing in it but a handkerchief and a few old bills, and Lord knows there's more where they came from . . ."

A receipted bill, from a public utility, perhaps . . . would that do for identification at a bank? Elizabeth didn't know. She said, "Yes, it belonged to Mrs. Bennett, who used to take care of the children. She lost it here and we combed the house . . . where did you find it, Noreen?" and knew the answer to that even before the girl spoke.

"In the closet in my room, way up on the shelf at the back. I did some Christmas shopping this morning and when I put the presents away I felt it there. . . . I hope Mrs. Bennett remembers just what was in it," said Noreen, her colour high, "because I never touched it at all, Mrs. March, except to bring it straight down to you."

She gave her head a quick perplexed shake and gazed troubledly down at the bag. This, thought Elizabeth, must be the perpetual nightmare of people working in other people's houses. She said quickly, "Of course not," and then, "Thanks, Noreen. I'll take care of it."

So the errand of the intruder in Noreen's room yesterday was explained. The pocketbook had not been in the closet when Noreen moved her things in; Mrs. Bennett had given the room a thorough turning-out and Elizabeth herself had inspected it. The placing of it there could only be a safeguard, an ace in the hole if the matter of the forged cheques should ever come under open discussion. How logically the suggestion of searching Noreen's room could be presented . . .

And it might have worked if Elizabeth

hadn't seen the face in the window, the face that was not Noreen's. It was a purely negative identification but none the less certain for that: if you saw something jarringly wrong, and were only allowed a fleeting instant, you couldn't assign it to its proper background. You could only know that it was out of context.

What had it been in the case of the face in the window — height, contour, quality of movement?

Elizabeth took the pocketbook to her room and examined it. Mrs. Bennett had been accurate; there was a handkerchief, a horn hairpin, a two-cent stamp, a plumber's bill. It told her nothing except the manner of its arrival in the house.

Sitting there on the edge of her bed, Elizabeth knew with a feeling that was half dread and half relief that the time had come to tell Oliver about the forged cheques.

When you knew about the cheques, Jeep's spoiled birthday and the destruction of the roses fell into a different focus. It might have been argued, before, that the cheques themselves were a simple, not-uncommon case of theft — but then there would have been no stranger in Noreen's room, and Mrs. Bennett's bag would have been disposed of.

It was nearly five o'clock. Elizabeth put the

black purse in a drawer of her bureau and went downstairs.

Constance met her in the lower hall. "Oh, here you are. I was just coming up. There's cold chicken in the icebox and I've fixed a salad and made some strawberry shortcake. I thought I'd tell you because," said Constance, flushing like an elderly schoolgirl, "I won't be in to dinner tonight."

Elizabeth swallowed her surprise. Of course — H. W., who must be following up his gift of perfume. She smiled involuntarily at her cousin's retreating back and went out to look at the kitchen clock. With her decision to tell Oliver about the cheques, the time until he came home seemed suddenly endless and empty.

Noreen was heating *consommé* and cutting *croûtons;* she turned to smile at Elizabeth and then at Maire. "Tell Mama what you saw this afternoon."

"A buffalo," said Maire, radiant.

"Maire!"

Maire turned her face away from Noreen's reproachful gaze and addressed herself importantly to Elizabeth. The buffalo dwindled and then disappeared as she lost interest; they had, it turned out, seen ducks instead, and Jeep had cried all the way home.

Elizabeth said seriously, "He's little, he gets

tired," and, "Come to think of it, where is Jeep?"

Jeep was in the small back L of the kitchen, peacefully oiling his tricycle with mustard, from which he was separated with great difficulty. Noreen set the table for their supper and pointed out the possibilities of the *croûtons*. Elizabeth left them in an absorbed silence and went into the living-room to wait for Oliver.

He would believe her now, because he had to; the watchful impersonal look would go out of his eyes. If there were someone else who understood, someone else to watch the narrow line between normality and disaster, then she could stand it. She could stand anything as long as Oliver was with her, as he would be, as he couldn't help being. . . .

It was five-thirty and then a quarter to six, and Elizabeth dropped all pretence of reading and walked nervously up and down the length of the room, cupping her hands against her eyes to stare out into the dark. The children finished their supper and followed Noreen upstairs for their bath, and Oliver still had not come. . . . Elizabeth went on pacing.

Her own reflection in a mirror caught and stopped her. Pale pointed face, emptied of its assurance, filled with inner questions. No colour at all in her cheeks, her lips, just the startlingly dark arch of brows and etching of lashes around frightened eyes.

It wouldn't do under Oliver's new clinical gaze. She ran upstairs. The children were splashing in the tub, and there was a line of light under Constance's bedroom door. In their own bathroom Elizabeth washed her face in icy water, put a flick of powder over the resultant pink, used her lipstick. She looked better now — still not like a seasoned mother of two, not like the Elizabeth March looking tiltedly out of her book jackets — but better.

There was the doorbell; was Oliver locked out, or was it the telephone? Elizabeth opened the bedroom door and listened, and heard the rustle of bath water and a shouted "That's MY duck." And something else. Oliver's voice.

His car must have driven in just as she had gone up the stairs. Elizabeth went along the hall and stopped with her foot on the top step of the stairs and her call frozen in her throat. Below her, beyond the curve of the banister railing, Oliver said softly and concentratedly,

"Friday noon. Same place . . . ? Right. And look, for God's sake, I told you — don't call me here again."

He said 'Right' again, but Elizabeth only half-heard that and didn't hear the click of the receiver at all.

# 7

"Windy out," said Oliver, "and getting cold as the devil. Shall we have a fire? Yes, we shall."

His topcoat and the evening paper went haphazardly into a chair. He knelt at the fireplace, saying casually over his shoulder, "Where is everybody? Kids in bed?"

Elizabeth clasped her cold hands tightly together behind her back. "About to be. . . . Did the phone ring just now, or was I hearing things?"

Oliver balanced logs and struck a match. He said cheerfully, standing again, "It did. Wrong number." The kindling and newspaper blazed high, and waves of light washed concealingly over his face. "Drink? . . ."

That was what bothered Elizabeth most of all — the easy good humour he hadn't shown for weeks. As though the telephone call and his Friday appointment had transformed him; as though lying to her, idly, expertly, gave the thing an extra fillip. She was glad the firelight masked her own face; she could feel her cheeks burning with shock. That was odd, because her hands and her feet and the very centre of herself felt so deadly, bitterly cold.

They had cocktails, and Constance came downstairs wearing a soft green suit Elizabeth hadn't seen before. The lines of it took the heaviness away from her body; the colour made her skin and hair years younger. Constance, fidgeting, examining the seams of her gloves minutely, seemed vaguely embarrassed over her own changed appearance.

Presently headlights glimmered through the gap in the hedge. Elizabeth and Oliver, realizing simultaneously that the driver was not going to emerge, broke politely into small talk while Constance put on her coat and went to the door. There she said breathlessly, "I've got my key. . . . Good night," and let herself out into the windy dark.

"Don't wait up, Ma," murmured Oliver, catching Elizabeth's eyes. "Isn't this something new?"

Elizabeth answered that with a shrug. She set the table and lighted candles; in the kitchen she tasted Constance's salad dressing and added salt and a few drops of vinegar. She moved about automatically, and went on listening to the memory of Oliver's voice.

'I told you — don't call me here again.' She

had been discussed, warned against; she was, intolerably, the female in the oldest, shabbiest tag-line of all: If a woman answers, hang up.

And at the other end of the wire, whose voice?

Friday noon, same place. It sounded like the essence of all clandestine meetings; it sounded as alien to Oliver as the heavy exotic perfume had seemed in Noreen's bedroom. And it sounded like a warning bell that this was a part of what she feared.

In the living-room again, she remembered all at once what had been driven out of her mind by the telephone call. Friday was the date of her morning appointment with Hathaway. It was a long-established hour that she always took when possible, because it meant she could meet Oliver for lunch before driving home. She said casually, "Oh, by the way, can we lunch Friday? Hathaway's seeing me at eleven, and I'll be through in plenty of time."

"Good," said Oliver promptly. "Dinty Moore's?"

She met his gaze squarely, and it looked pleased and inquiring. "Yes, let's," she said, turning away. Friday would tell her a great deal, Friday was the fork in the road. . . .

They had dinner in comparative silence until Oliver reached for a cigarette and said mildly, "Constance made any New Year's resolutions that you know of?"

Elizabeth took fire instantly. "Such as what?"

"Such as plans," Oliver said, still mild. "Don't think I don't appreciate what she's done, because I do. But if we're to be a permanent unit of five instead of four I think we ought to know about it and arrange things accordingly."

Five instead of four; it wasn't a felicitous phrase. Oliver, knowing it, said almost without pausing, "What I mean is that if she's staying we'd better make it known that where we're asked, she is, and so forth. What we've got here is, if you'll pardon my saying so, a very half-assed arrangement, indeed."

"And what would you suggest?" inquired Elizabeth, unreasonably angry. "That I tell her we don't need her any more, and to go and buy a one-way ticket to someplace?"

"Damn it, no," said Oliver. "You know perfectly well what I mean."

But I don't, thought Elizabeth; that's just the trouble. I don't know whether you want us to be alone again or whether you're afraid of Constance, because she's my cousin, watching and recording with those eyes of hers. She said stiffly, "I'll get coffee, shall I?" and escaped.

It was after coffee, it was nearly nine o'clock when Maire's scream rang through the quiet house.

To Elizabeth it was the sudden black eruption of everything hidden and malign in the house. She felt one burning wave of panic from head to foot and then she was on the stairs and running before Oliver had had time to do more than start to his feet and say, "Take it easy —"

Maire screamed again as Elizabeth reached the upper hall and brushed blindly past Noreen, bathrobed and blinking. She flung open the door of the children's room, her breath shaking, and saw them both there and safe, Jeep humped like a camel in his crib, Maire sitting up in a tumble of bedclothes.

She was only half awake. Elizabeth went to her and put a reassuring arm around the small pyjamaed shoulders. She couldn't have controlled her voice a moment ago; now it came out softly, just above a whisper. "It's all right, honey — back under the blankets. . . ."

Maire murmured something and crawled under the covers, and Elizabeth, smoothing them, looked around the room. Closet door closed, curtains stirring in the faint draught of cold air from the window — the child had waked and seen that, probably, like a dream brought to frightening life. . . .

Branches scraped against the porch roof. Elizabeth, looking up from the watchfully open eye above the level of the blankets, saw the huge soft shadow on the far wall and turned her head sharply. It was Noreen, who had kept a silent vigil in the doorway, who must have seen Elizabeth's nervous, roving inspection of the room.

Maire's visible eye had closed, lashes firmly down on the round cheek. Elizabeth stood up and moved away from the bed, and Noreen whispered practically, "Perhaps that draught — ?"

There was no direct draught on either of the children, they were both aware of that, and equally aware that the window that was open led on to the low porch roof, against which the apple tree, jostling in the night wind, made a perfect natural ladder. Elizabeth knew that in the odd little silence during which they stood facing each other in the cool stirring half-dark, had it borne in on her even more strongly when Noreen tiptoed past her, closed the window over the porch and opened the other, the one at the foot of Maire's bed, fractionally, from the top.

Noreen must feel it too, then — the gentle, intentional warping in the house. She wasn't a fool, and she had seen the roses, the bon-bons, Mrs. Bennett's purse — most important of all, she was an outsider, looking in. And knowing, or suspecting, so that she grew daily more shadowy-eyed and apprehensive.

Talk to her, thought Elizabeth, suddenly alert; pin down, if possible, small facts of timing and opportunity that might have escaped her in her own fog of dread. . . .

Downstairs, Oliver was turning out all but the living-room lights, to be left on for Constance. He glanced at her briefly. "Early to bed, whether you like it or not — you're shot, in case you didn't know."

Elizabeth said nothing; she picked up her book and cigarettes and went silently upstairs. She was in bed when Oliver sauntered out of the bathroom, toothbrush suspended, and said, "What was all the shouting about — bad dream?"

"I suppose so."

Oliver disappeared again; after an interval of splashing, next-to-drowning sounds he was back again. "You know, some day," he said without inflection, "you're going to shoot up the stairs like that and trip and break your neck while Maire goes peacefully back to sleep."

Trip. And break her neck. While Maire . . . Elizabeth said tightly, "I can't help running when I — when anything, *anything* might happen in this house," and to her intense horror burst into tears.

Oliver was there instantly, much as she had been there for Maire, with close-holding arms and the safe steady shelter that everyone, child or adult, sought at times to grow quiet against. It took Elizabeth some time to grow quiet, because the accumulated terrors of six weeks came spilling and hiccupping out into Oliver's chest.

Even then, remembering the short hostile exchange over Constance, she held back the forged cheques, as though the unadmitted fear in her own mind put them in a place apart. She told Oliver, frantically, between sobs, about the roses: "I didn't, no matter what you think," about the bon-bons: "Can't you see how horribly deliberate that was?", about the face at Noreen's window: "I don't know who — and then the empty house. I'm so afraid," said Elizabeth unsteadily, lifting her head and staring blindly across the room. "I'm so terribly afraid."

Oliver's arms loosened. He was shaking his head, gently, as though he were afraid to trust himself with any more violent gesture. When she stopped speaking he tilted her face and said, "Elizabeth . . ." and groaned and gave his head a quick clearing shake and started again, gazing intently down at her. "You mean you've been living with this — this business ever since that mess over the roses?

94

When you said yourself that —"

Elizabeth was queerly, instantly conscious of the importance of this. "When I said what?"

But Oliver shook his head, listening. Footsteps went discreetly down the hall, a light switch clicked, a door closed.

Constance.

"Oh, God," Elizabeth said bleakly. "That does it up nicely."

"That," said Oliver, grim, "is what I meant. Here, let's have a cigarette and go at this a little at a time. . . ."

Elizabeth stopped listening after the first few quiet words, realizing what seemed just then the ultimate horror. She had told it all to Oliver, gasping and crying and shaking like a child — and Oliver was treating her like a child, to whom he might explain kindly that the shadow under her bed was her slipper.

No way out there, no one to help her after all. . . .

She pulled stiffly away from Oliver as he concluded, ". . . Ten to one I'm right. And things always look different in the morning — worse, maybe, but different. What you need at the moment is about twelve hours' sleep."

Elizabeth lifted her bent head and caught an astonishing glimpse of herself in her dressing-table mirror. Wild eyes, wet cheeks, recklessly ruffled hair . . . no wonder Oliver thought she was hysterical.

Or did he merely pretend to think so?

Oliver was in the mirror, too, his gaze thoughtful and far away. As though her eyes on his reflection had burned him he stood up and crossed to the bureau. "Think you could swallow a pill?"

"All of them."

"Come now," said Oliver, his back to her, "I wouldn't —" His voice stopped, and Elizabeth glanced up at the sharp-edged silence. "Aren't they there?"

"Got them," said Oliver, and brought her the capsule and a glass of water.

Elizabeth settled herself under the covers and caught Oliver at the edge of his bed. "Do you suppose Constance locked the front door?"

"Probably."

"I wish you'd look."

As soon as he had left the room resignedly, Elizabeth slid out of bed and crossed to the bureau. When Oliver came back she was in bed again, composed, still, with nothing to show the violent pounding at her temples.

Two capsules left in the little grey pasteboard box that, last night, had held nine. Oliver knew it, because he had got the capsule the night before.

Six missing.

You'll trip and break your neck, said the shocked hammering of her blood.

And: What are we going to do about Elizabeth?

# 8

It could have been two o'clock or four when
Elizabeth found herself awake, nudged out of
sleep by a change in the texture of the icy,
deep-night silence.

A bar of moonlight hung like a knife across
the front of the bureau; she could almost have
screamed at that. When the orientation of
pulse and brain and senses was complete, she
knew it was nothing in the room that had
waked her. The curtains hung straight and
still, the moonlight might have been a painted
thing, across from her Oliver slept undis-
turbed, a long scissoring shape under blankets. She had dropped her head uneasily to
the pillow again when she heard the soft, the
indescribably secret sound.

She knew later that a louder sound must
have preceded it, jarring her out of the depths
of exhaustion. Because this would never have
waked her, this gentle and almost snuffling
sound from somewhere below her in the
house. As though — she listened again and

found it in the immense library of connected sounds stored by the mind for random use. It was the faint shudder of wood being pushed, the delicate answer of metal.

Someone was trying the front door.

But Oliver had gone down and made very sure of the lock. *Hadn't he?*

The back door, the cellar door with its other entrance into the kitchen; the porch door — open to a seeking hand at this unconscious hour? Her shoulders and throat ached from the steady stubborn lift of her head as she listened. Elizabeth realized all at once that the sound had stopped and wouldn't come again.

The floor was cold under her bare feet as she stepped off the rugs in her progress to the window. It was a stage-set lawn: bare arching trees, lawn drifted with shadows, stone path glimmering faintly with frost. Only the hedge moved at the inner edges of its opening, as though it had been disturbed a bare second ago — or had she imagined that?

"Can't you sleep?" said Oliver's voice, shooting unexpectedly out of the dark.

How long had he been awake, how long had he watched her? Elizabeth answered at random and went back to bed, still listening acutely. She was almost asleep when she heard the small, infinitely careful closing of

Noreen Delaney's door.

Morning. Maire running a slight fever. Constance preoccupied over her generous, post-Oliver breakfast, going away behind her pale folded eyelids so that Elizabeth, fidgeting nervously with her coffee, felt as though she were excusing herself needlessly when she rose and went out to the kitchen.

Maire was making a bubbling hum in her orange juice, Jeep wore a cereal beard. Elizabeth smiled at them both and said, "Noreen, if you have a minute I'd like to talk to you."

Noreen had just poured the children's milk into cups in the pantry. Elizabeth watched with mild astonishment the narrow shoulders, the small deft hands, go rigid. After a second the hands went down automatically to the apron, twisting there, and the girl turned. She said on a caught breath, "Mrs. March, that's what I've been wanting to ask you. If there's something I should be doing that I'm not doing . . . it's hard to know in a new place, and I've been wondering — I know you had someone so satisfactory before me —"

"It's not that at all," Elizabeth interrupted hastily. "We're more than satisfied, Noreen, it's something else I wanted to talk to you about."

How pale the girl was, how braced . . . was

100

it apprehension over her job, or a deeper fear? Elizabeth met the grave green-brown eyes, shadowed in mauve down to the ridge of cheekbone. The shadows were new; Noreen hadn't had those when she first came, nor the faltering look to the young, down-curving mouth.

She knew something — or she was afraid of something. Elizabeth was startled into changing her tack; she said gently, "Are you quite sure you like it here, Noreen? Don't be embarrassed to say so if you don't — children this age are quite an undertaking."

"Oh, please, Mrs. March, I love the children!" It was soft; it had an underlying violence, and Elizabeth was startled again. Noreen gave her a small anxious smile, and Maire said curiously, "Who loves the chillrin?" and that, temporarily, was the end of it.

In the middle of Friday morning Elizabeth dressed with foolish, superstitious haste. Her plum-blue suit, the fitted stiff-skirted rosy tweed coat that wasn't really warm enough for a bitter day like this but might deceive Hathaway's bright and nonchalant eye. She felt like a mad reversal of Lot's wife, as though the danger lay in looking forward to the ring of the telephone and Oliver's voice saying regretfully that he couldn't meet her for lunch.

She had been braced all through breakfast, but all Oliver said was, "Call me from the office there when you're through, and I'll give you a head start and meet you in the bar at Dinty Moore's."

"Where you will take a head start." She had felt gay with relief because Oliver was breaking his soft, hurried telephone appointment in order to meet her. There had been an obscure choice to make, and he had made it in her favour. Why look anxiously at the clock, then, why want so urgently to be out of the house and on her way to Boston before anything could happen . . . ?

The telephone rang at nine-thirty and it was Brenda McCollum to ask them to an eggnog party on Christmas Eve; Elizabeth said they would love to but were busy. It rang again at five minutes to ten.

Oliver said, "Damn it, of all days. Moulton's called an eleven-thirty conference. I'd like to sneak out the back way, but —"

"You can't, of course not," Elizabeth said, carefully bright. "Oh well, the skies won't fall. Have a nice meeting."

"Isn't that too bad," said Constance abstractedly, glancing up from the desk in the living-room. "Oliver's tied up, is he?"

"So it seems. I'll see you later, or rather

sooner," Elizabeth said, and closed the front door behind her and walked down the lawn to her car.

Oliver had calculated the time to a nicety, he hadn't pricked the bubble an instant too soon. It was a pity he had told her only a few days ago about Moulton's extended West-coast trip. Otherwise it might have sounded like the truth.

Hathaway saw her early and said with emphasis that she looked frightful; what was she trying to do to herself? Elizabeth sat in a fever of impatience while he asked questions, stared at her brightly, and at length wrote notes and a prescription. The taxi she called came instantly, and it was just ten minutes to twelve when they pulled in at the curb opposite Oliver's office building.

She leaned forward. "Driver, I'm meeting someone here and we're going on. It shouldn't be more than a few minutes."

Noon, Oliver had said to the unknown voice on the telephone two days ago. And he would have to get wherever he was going. Elizabeth watched the stream of lunch-hour traffic at the mouth of the International Chemical building, half-hoping that Oliver would not emerge at all, knowing coldly that he would.

103

Even then, at seven minutes to twelve, she might have missed him if it hadn't been for a snarl in the sidewalk traffic caused by a lost and bewildered French poodle. In the small island of space made by veering pedestrians, Oliver appeared between the gilt-grilled doors of the grey marble lobby, halted briefly to cup his hands around a match and started up the block. Elizabeth watched him without feeling anything at all.

He was going to cross the street, he was hailing the cab at the corner. Elizabeth clasped her hands tightly together in her lap and made a decision she hadn't consciously considered, perhaps because she hadn't wanted to look closely at it. She leaned forward again to the driver. "Oh, we've missed each other. It's that red and yellow cab up ahead, Driver. If you'll follow that . . ."

"The one that fella just got in?" said the driver baldly.

"Yes." She was stony with not caring. He had probably waited like this often, with women checking up on their husbands, men checking up on their wives. She hadn't thought she could ever do that, but the odd part of it was that at the last minute everything whittled down to the simple necessity of knowing. What to do when you knew was something else again, and not even the most

104

knowledgeable taxi driver could help you there. . . .

Oliver's cab led them into a part of Boston Elizabeth didn't know and wouldn't have been able to find again. She had stared at the red and yellow fenders ahead so long that she had stopped seeing them, and she was startled when the driver said laconically, "There goes your friend," and drew in to the curb.

She had had change ready; she dropped it into his outstretched palm and was out of the cab without ever having seen his face at all.

# 9

Revolving doors carried Oliver out of sight. With an instinctive caution she hadn't known she possessed, Elizabeth waited until a balding mink-faced man in a trench coat had followed him before she walked up the three shallow steps and spun her way into the lobby of the Hotel Savoia.

She couldn't have said exactly how the Savoia ticketed itself, but it did. It might have been the general amber gloom, lighted at cautious intervals by a pink silk lamp, or the lounging bellboy whose eyes roved over her with a kind of bored speculation; it might have been the blonde seated with improbable hauteur just beside the elevators or the slumbrous silence that pervaded the whole lobby. She had thought herself numb and too driven to care, but her instant and violent distaste was so strong that it was an effort to remember why she was here, and to find Oliver in the dimness.

To her right were a Western Union counter

and a bookstall, directly opposite her, across an area of small couches and chairs with a few unwinking occupants, were the elevators and an alcove lined with public telephones. At the end of the lobby to her left, Oliver's head and shoulders rose out of a giant rubber plant at the desk. Elizabeth advanced a little; he was talking to the room clerk, and then bending his head intently.

How had she ever thought this room was dim? It seemed suddenly floodlit without shadow or shelter from the countless stares, sharp as drawn knives, that had found her face, slyly, without her knowing it. The woman in the bookstall, the clerk at the Western Union barrier, the lounging bellboy, the blonde beside the elevators, a spinsterish man on the nearest sofa — their eyes pinned her against a wall of light, dissecting, cataloguing. It was the old, old dream of suddenly discovering in the midst of the assembly hall that you had no clothes on, but it was not a dream. Briefly, Elizabeth hated Oliver for the mere fact of bringing her here.

In another instant she would have to bolt and run . . . shakily, she pushed back a glove and pretended an oblivious glance at her watch. She couldn't read its face, but the small gesture shattered the spell. The male spinster began to tweak his nose nervously, the blonde readjusted her hemline, the woman in the bookstall turned her back — but in the interval Oliver had left the desk and was walking rapidly across the lobby toward the elevators.

She could still have escaped, she could have fled out into the winter sunlight, hoping to find a remnant of the pride she had had to shed at the door. But then she would have shed it for nothing. . . . No. Find out what there was to know, what there was to fight — or, indeed, if victory would be a little more intolerable than loss.

Elizabeth did what no power on earth could have forced her to do ten seconds ago: she walked briskly across the lobby, passing within two feet of Oliver and the group of people leaving the elevator, and stood in front of the telephone book on a chain in line with the elevators, so that his back was half turned to her. It crossed her mind wryly that it was helpful in situations like this to know your husband's habits. Oliver would give his floor number as he entered the elevator . . . but would he, here?

"Six," said Oliver, startlingly close by.

Six. No good at all, unless . . . The uniformed boy had stepped out of the elevator and was waiting for more passengers. A man and woman Elizabeth hadn't seen before were crossing the lobby. The blonde stood up, gave her a curious glance and followed them into the elevator. The doors closed and they were gone. Elizabeth walked to the elevators and pressed the button and was rewarded instantly. It was the second elevator down, and the operator was benign and white-haired. "Six, ma'am. Getting colder, isn't it? Looks as if we might have snow for Christmas after all."

Elizabeth said that it did, and stepped out on six. Her heart was pounding; for a wild instant she confused that with the faint rapid sound of footsteps in one of the near corridors. Oliver's walk, quick, unerring . . .

She was up a short stem of corridor, and she was in luck; as she stood at the point of intersection, motion at the far end of the hall to her right caught her eye. She turned her head just in time to see Oliver disappearing behind a door that closed quietly after him.

Silence again, dimly busy with the echo of traffic. From somewhere close by sounded a heavy crash of glass, and a woman's voice said stormily, "Ox!" All Elizabeth's detachment dropped away, and she was acutely, incredulously aware of her errand in this furtive, pink-lit hotel. Not an automaton after all, not a woman she would have felt sorry and a little embarrassed about, but herself, Elizabeth

March. In search of the shabbiest possible information about her husband, and finding it.

She forced herself up the corridor Oliver had taken, and looked at the room number. This was reality; it would be difficult, later, convincing herself of that. She wondered whether she would ever be able to forget the grey light from the window striking waterily across the numerals, or the little triangular chip in the paint just above them. Then she walked quickly away.

The room clerk watched her as she approached the desk; had he noticed her earlier across the lobby, seen her waiting, entering the elevator so urgently? The rose-red coat flared like a candle in the dusk; she was conscious of an automatic lift of eyes as she passed.

He listened attentively while, deliberately vague, she told him about a friend of a friend registered at the hotel. She believed the number of the room was 619, and the name — she had trouble finding one in the confusion of her mind — was Hunt.

The clerk gazed at her sardonically. "Sorry, madam. There's no one by that name registered here at the moment."

"Oh, but there must be." She was on firmer ground now that they both knew he didn't believe her. "I'm quite sure she said the Savoia, Room 619. Would you," she stared coolly back at him, "mind checking, please."

The clerk sighed audibly and turned to ruffle through a slender stack of cards. He withdrew one and held it a little apart from the others; when he faced her again, Elizabeth, every nerve bared, saw instantly the subtle change in his manner.

A frond of the rubber plant quivered near her cheek. The clerk said with a kind of suave enjoyment, "Room 619 is occupied by a C. G. Massman. Sorry."

He had dropped the 'Madam' pointedly, he was dismissing her with his eyes, his tone, a careless turn of his shoulder. "Alfred. Did Mr. Casales speak to you . . ."

Elizabeth walked away, on fire with fury at herself, at Oliver, at the knowing impudence that seemed to saturate the air. She didn't know what prompted her to look back. The room clerk had his elbows on the desk, confiding in an antique bellboy who was watching her retreat with a wrinkled, appreciative grin.

They all know a joke when they see one at the Savoia, Elizabeth thought, feeling the grin like a scald on her back. Damn you, Oliver, for every minute of this . . .

She clung to her anger as she would have

clung to a spar, because under it waited the yawning and bottomless fear.

It was bitterly cold, driving home. She kept herself fiercely from thinking, because there wasn't room in her mind for both traffic and shock. She reached the house at about two o'clock and found it empty and mockingly serene.

A match to the living-room fire, a cup of scalding tea — and then, inescapably, the facts. What, after all, did she know? That Oliver had made an obscure appointment by telephone and warned his caller to secrecy; that he had lied to her in order to keep the appointment, that it had had to be kept in a bedroom in a shady side-street hotel, under arrangements so blatant that even the hotel employees were amused.

That — because it came down to this — in the short space of not quite two months her life had gone casually to pieces.

Was it possible that all this was unconnected, that Oliver was so carried away by another woman that he had forgotten all his latent fastidiousness, his dislike of marital murk?

If that were true, then her marriage was as good as dissolved, because even if she could manage to go on living with Oliver, she could not possibly live with herself.

If it were not true — and it was that sliver of incredulity that had persuaded her to follow Oliver from his office — then he was caught in the same delicate mesh of malevolence that was spinning itself about everything she loved.

*Why?*

Constance, arriving in a little flurry of cold air, seemed mildly surprised to find her back. "I thought you might spend the afternoon in town, you go in so seldom. Have you been home long?"

"Only a few minutes." Elizabeth watched her cousin removing her gloves, putting the finger tips and wrist edges meticulously in line, folding them away in her purse. Constance, she thought, was very like sand going through an hourglass, recording everything, affected by nothing. She said, "The children are out for a walk, I gather."

"I believe," Constance was vague, "that Noreen had promised them something about the pond. It's too bad, isn't it, that you couldn't have made your trip into town with Mrs. Brent."

Was there anything more than idleness in the thick-lidded eyes? No . . . *no.* Elizabeth flicked out a match with care. "I didn't know Lucy was going in."

"Oh, she may not have been. I picked up a few last-minute things in town just after you left, and when I saw her at the station I just assumed, for some reason . . . tell me," said Constance, "what did the doctor say?"

"What doctors usually say. Liver-and-iron and sleep."

"That's all?"

"Yes," said Elizabeth, surprised, and turned her head, in time to see Constance flushing as unhappily as though she had been caught making a face at Elizabeth's back. She said awkwardly, "I just . . . you've seemed so —" and Elizabeth, sorry for her and regretting her own crispness, said, "It was just the usual check-up. But I haven't been sleeping as well as I ought."

"Nerves," said Constance briskly, herself again. "Although I must say that for the last night or two I've been unusually wakeful myself. It's the wind, I think, it makes you hear things."

"We're quite exposed here," Elizabeth said, and thought with sudden dreariness how little it took to remind her of fear, of the night when the sounds at the door had not been the wind.

"I hadn't thought of it before," said Constance reflectively, starting for the stairs, "but you are quite exposed, aren't you, Elizabeth?"

Oliver asked her about the doctor, too, with a casual "Everything all right this morning?" when he got home that evening, with a subtly different tone up in their bedroom.

"What did Hathaway really say?"

"That I'm a little underweight and could use a few vitamins, but then," said Elizabeth, "doctors always like you round and rosy."

She could feel Oliver's waiting silence behind her; she could feel the mount of her own bitter surprise at the fact that he could make any reference at all to that morning. She took refuge in action, brushing her hair so vigorously that it hurt, seeing almost as clearly as her own reflection the uncrossable chasm that lay just under the surface between herself and Oliver.

Once he knew that she had followed him to the Savoia, once the knowledge of his deception was a shared and admitted thing, there could be no going back. An impulsive word from her would open the chasm — and no power on earth could close it again.

Part of the plan of whoever it was who hated her?

Oliver was leaning against his bureau, dark head bent, frowning down at the cuff-links he rattled like dice in his palm. "Hathaway didn't suggest your taking a vacation, getting away for a while?"

No mistaking the eagerness there, or the faint surprise, as though — Elizabeth had a flashing memory of Oliver at the telephone, severing a Boston connexion — he had asked Hathaway to put forth such a suggestion. He wouldn't have to worry about surreptitious calls, then, or awkwardly broken lunch dates — was that why he had inquired so restlessly about Constance's plans the other night?

She caught back a tumble of words; she thought clearly, The children. You aren't only yourself, you're the children too. And if you confront Oliver and he admits what you're afraid of and you make the only possible answer, you make it for Maire and Jeep too.

She said, "No, he didn't say anything about it," and, very casually, "Don't forget to pick up Maire's sled tomorrow, will you?"

Christmas Eve came with a dark and biting cold. Elizabeth hunted for the red candles and pinned up fragrant sprays of fir, dug through the attic for last year's lights and the treetop angel and didn't, in all the furious activity, escape the naked fear that walked with her all day long.

She had learned to dread the lulls, the pleasant normal times when everything she loved was safe and near her and anything else

116

was built of shadows. It was as though Christmas were a talisman, to be snatched from her; as though she were especially vulnerable on this of all days, and violence might burst forth at any moment among the flowers and firelight.

Noreen Delaney left at three o'clock, flushed and smiling and protesting at the presents Elizabeth put into her arms. Oliver departed to pick up the tree; Constance, restrainedly festive in brown satin, put on an apron and began to make *canapés*. Lucy and Steven Brent were coming for cocktails, and Elizabeth, trying grimly to ignore the web that bound them all together, had asked the Stockbridges and Bill and Ellie Seaver.

The children settled down to untangle an immense snarl of red satin ribbon, and Elizabeth joined Constance in the pantry and thought, Really, this is quite simple, and went back in the midst of the peaceful silence to find the white leather chair slipcovered in Christmas seals. Maire cried bitterly when they were removed; Jeep, philosophical, picked them up quietly as they were removed and transferred them to the wall.

Elizabeth sat them firmly down to listen to carols, and found that the small hushed faces and faraway eyes seemed like an invitation to malice, and frightened her more than ever.

By six o'clock she had them bathed and fed and in bed, with intense queries as to whether Santa Claus would come down the chimney when there was a fire burning in the fireplace. Elizabeth said gravely that they would put the fire out at once, and went into her own room to dress.

Not the satin-panelled black — she had worn it that other night when the Brents had come, and it still carried memories of shock. The copper faille, then, making a great deal of her white throat and very little of her waist, belling in crisp extravagant folds. She dressed; she went downstairs to find Oliver and Bill Seaver closeted in the pantry, making drinks, and Ellie Seaver, pink and gold and giddy, trapped bewilderedly in a conversation about tulips with Constance. At six-thirty the Stockbridges arrived, and the Brents.

Before they had all been there five minutes Elizabeth realized startledly that Lucy and Steven were at each other's throats, that Steven was gently and forlornly drunk and Lucy silkily furious. It was in the living-room like vapour. The Stockbridges were alert and fascinated, only taking themselves off reluctantly to meet a train; the Seavers, who knew the Brents less well, looked uncomfortable. Even Constance sat warily watching.

It wasn't anything they said to each other, it

was more like a quarrel that had been dropped at the gate and would be resumed on the doorstep . . . or was it only that? Wasn't there a new sharpness in Lucy, a triumphant interchange of glances as though a point were being settled?

It was, thought Elizabeth, tired and faintly angry, the worst possible thing that could happen to a party — and it was also very odd between Lucy and Steven. Out of habit she sought Oliver's eye and caught a quick, accomplished grimace. Even then, nothing happened until nearly seven-thirty, when the Seavers had left, and then it was like a spark introduced into a gas-filled room.

Upstairs, a door opened. Elizabeth started uneasily to her feet, listening to the soft little sounds of pyjamaed feet, and Oliver said from the couch, "It's Christmas Eve, we'll be getting this all night." She sank back again uncertainly, because from her chair she could see the stairs.

It was Maire who rounded the turn of the hall so cautiously, Maire in her pink pyjamas, her pale-gold head tousled and her eyes huge. She was so intent on her own tiptoeing progress that she didn't seem to notice Elizabeth's silent, instinctive rise. She reached the foot of the stairs and peered into the living-room, and she let out a wail of pure terror.

119

It wasn't the inarticulate howl of babyhood, it had a sound, a baying and stricken sound that was like the very definition of danger. "Oun . . . *Oun* . . ."

Elizabeth ran to her and caught the small trembling body close. She didn't know whether the panic had communicated itself or whether her own dreadful shaking had leaped to meet the cry that went plunging and echoing through her, like a stranger identifying himself at last.

# 10

*Oun.*

It was evil, unearthly, seeming to contain its own frightened echo. To Elizabeth it was peculiarly terrifying, as though Maire, with the simplicity of childhood, had managed to put a name to the lurking visitant in the house.

She found, when she came downstairs again, that the living-room was still charged with it. Lucy said curiously, "Does she do that often?" and Oliver: "All quiet?" Constance murmured mildly about the effect of Santa Claus on infant minds. Steven Brent looked up from an intent study of his shoe-tops and said, "The odd and unflattering part of it is that it seemed to be something she saw down here."

Elizabeth, still shaken, was startled at that — she had thought no one but herself had noticed Maire's swift wide stare down the room before she began to scream. Was it here, then, here in the room with her, hiding and triumphant . . . ?

This was ghastly.

"Clown," Constance was saying thoughtfully, as though Steven hadn't spoken. "Some confusion, perhaps, with the stereotyped Santa Claus face?"

"Owl," Lucy offered hopefully. "You know, night creatures . . ."

Night creatures. Fumbling at the door in darkness, waking a child to terror, working tirelessly toward the tumbling-down of her own existence . . . Elizabeth had begun to tremble again. She crossed to the fire and picked up the tongs and made an effort at casualness, saying over her shoulder, "It's so hard to tell when they're Maire's age. . . ."

It seemed a lifetime, although it was only another drink, before the Brents left and an exchange of Merry Christmases hung on the damp icy air. After dinner Constance retired to make mince pies by her mother's unparalleled recipe, and Elizabeth and Oliver began to trim the tree. Oliver had apparently been waiting for seclusion; he said, dumping ropes of tinsel unceremoniously out of a box, "That was a hell of a thing, wasn't it, Maire's bursting out like that? Bad dream, I suppose, or getting all wound up over tomorrow."

He made it a statement, but he was watching her. Elizabeth hung a red bulb with care. "I don't know. But it's what she said before."

"When?"

"The other night, when she woke up crying, I thought then that it was just the beginning or the end of something she'd been dreaming about. But," said Elizabeth, scrupulously matter-of-fact, "she wasn't dreaming tonight."

Oliver's hands stopped briefly among the glistening ropes of tinsel. "You mean you think she's afraid of something — definite?"

Definite. What would a child of three and a half consider definite, and why was she herself so sure that Maire had seen something badly, frighteningly wrong? Because she was; so sure that when she thought about it like this, the little cluster of silver and sea-green bulbs she was holding wasn't safe in her fingers. She put it down and looked at Oliver. She said, "Yes, in her own mind."

It wasn't quite honest, but being honest with Oliver lately had only increased the distance between them. Oliver looked relieved. "It'll probably turn out to be something in one of her books."

And maybe it would; maybe the wariness, the feeling of dread weren't justified at all this time. Elizabeth began to concentrate on her side of the tree, and stepped back at last to look at it. For an instant, with night at the windows and all the lights on, it was really Christmas Eve. The tree stood dripping and flashing in the corner, its bulbs glimmering through a mesh of silver. Even with the discarded boxes and cartons piled on the rug, it had a magical look, as though it actually had been dressed by a midnight visitor.

"Not bad," said Oliver. "In fact, one of our better trees. I'd better see if the lights work."

They did. Elizabeth gazed at the shining fragrant tree and thought of Maire and Jeep sleeping soundly upstairs and felt her heart tighten. She said, "I'll do the stockings if you'll put the presents out," and turned away.

Constance made coffee and admired the tree and insisted on using the carpet sweeper. At ten minutes after twelve, when they were all sitting in a bemused and exhausted silence, she rose, said practically, "Well — it's Christmas. I think I'll say goodnight," and started for the stairs. Surprisingly, because she was not demonstrative, she answered Elizabeth's "Merry Christmas, Constance," with a sudden awkward kiss on the cheek.

"The same to you, Elizabeth. Try to get a good sleep, you'll need all your energy tomorrow."

Was she saying more than the words themselves? Elizabeth was too tired to wonder. When Constance had gone she took a last slow look around the living-room, at the two fat red socks dangling from the mantel, the piled presents, gay with ribbon and seals and mystery. Maire's sled, leaning against the wall beside the tree, threw a long shadow; a bell on Jeep's fire truck caught the light winkingly. She said, "I suppose we'd better get to bed, the children will think it's morning any minute now," and stretched out a hand to her lamp.

"Right," said Oliver. "Thank God we don't have to leave by way of the chimney." He turned out lights and locked the doors and folded a stubborn red ember under ashes in the fireplace. Elizabeth realized belatedly that he had finished and was waiting beside her chair. She said, "Oh — ready?" and stood up.

They were very close together. Oliver put his hands on her shoulders and gazed at her gently and examiningly. "Still thinking about this 'oun' business, aren't you? That was a damned fool thing for Steven to say, about Maire seeing something down here to frighten her. You didn't" — were his fingers tightening, or did she imagine it? — "take him seriously, by any chance?"

It might have been the dimness, or Oliver's hands, or her own complete weariness that made her answer seem all at once important. Elizabeth stepped back, and was shocked at the sharpness of her own involuntary movement. She said, "It's much too late to take

125

anything seriously, except sleep. Coming?"

"Because," said Oliver as though he hadn't heard her and as though it had just occurred to him, "Noreen will be back tomorrow night, and chances are she knows all about this thing, whatever it is."

Yes, thought Elizabeth; almost certainly she knows — but can she be made to tell?

. . . There was a crowd gathered, and a great deal of clamour . . . was it fire? When she started forward to see, something soft and cloaking was flung over her eyes. She was not meant to see, then, she was to he kept from ever finding out — but she must find out. Elizabeth fought grimly with the softness against her face, and opened her eyes and looked into Jeep's, two inches away.

The clamour became Maire, crying, "Daddy, Mama and Daddy, come and look! Santa Claus came!" Jeep retrieved the slip she had flung off and put it on the pillow beside her face again and said, nodding his head earnestly, "You put this on, Mama." He sounded cajoling and patient, as though he had been saying it for some time, and Elizabeth sat up sleepily against her pillow.

It was Christmas morning.

In the other bed, Oliver stirred. Maire said triumphantly: "He's awake. Are you awake,

126

Daddy? Santa Claus came!"

Jeep was making small trotting side trips; a stocking and one black pump joined the heap on Elizabeth's pillow. With each delivery he said hopefully, "You put this on, Mama," and nodded and went off for more.

Oliver lifted his head, glanced at the clock and looked wryly across at Elizabeth. "Ten to six. Good God!"

"Not bad for Christmas morning."

"Don't you think so?" Oliver struggled up on his elbows and took a wider survey of the situation. After a moment he said kindly, "Why don't you children go back to bed for a while?"

Elizabeth couldn't help laughing at the gaping faces. "Daddy's joking. With tears in his eyes."

"Worth a try," said Oliver. "Oh well. Maire, hand me my bathrobe like a good girl. Look at Jeep, he's got your mother practically dressed."

The children finished opening their presents at last. Rubber animals and books and a Raggedy Ann, jack-in-the-boxes, Maire's set of tiny dishes lay mingled and for the moment unfought-over in a sea of ribbon and paper. Elizabeth and Oliver, fortified by coffee, looked at each other and smiled briefly. The children's Christmas had been a success, so much so that they were lost and faraway in delight, and unaware of being watched at all.

Constance came briskly in with a wastebasket, and Elizabeth said quickly, "Oh, let's leave it for a while, Constance, it looks so lavish." Constance sat down again with a faintly pained smile, but the wastebasket stayed there in a corner, waiting soberly to dispose of Christmas, to swallow up the festive litter.

"Shall we open ours?" Elizabeth always felt ridiculously shy and embarrassed at this point. When Oliver nodded she said, "You and Constance start. I'll get more coffee for all of us."

The morning was full of pale sunshine, the kitchen smelled pleasantly of coffee. Elizabeth groped for cigarettes in the pocket of her housecoat and waited for the percolator to heat. She was pouring the first cup when there was a bubbling shout from the living-room, Maire's usual spilling-over of amusement. "Daddy, you look funny in that!"

"Well, I don't know," Oliver was saying solemnly. "Think it's a little low-cut for me?"

Elizabeth put the percolator down and went inside to find Oliver eyeing a tumble of ice-green silk. She said, "That's for Constance. How on earth did I —" and behind her Constance said mildly, "I think I've got something of Oliver's here, haven't I?"

She held up a pair of ivory-backed military brushes, and looked at the card in her lap. Elizabeth looked too, and saw her own slanting dark-blue hand: "Constance from E." Just as the card with the nightgown had said, "Oliver from E."

She had made a mistake, even though the boxes and the wrappings were so different. But she watched, wondering, vaguely disturbed, while Constance undid a long narrow package. The card, slipped under green satin ribbon, said in Elizabeth's writing, "Constance from Oliver."

Constance pulled back tissue. There was a full pause, and then she said with forced animation, "Aren't they pretty. And very warm too, I imagine." .

It was a pair of black crocheted wool slippers, frankly giddy, with tiny sequined tassels. You might, thought Elizabeth remotely, as easily imagine Constance in a G-string. She put her hands to cheeks gone suddenly hot and said, "Oh, God. Then what did I give Noreen?"

They were both staring at her, Constance politely puzzled, Oliver incredulous. Even the children had noticed the sudden flat silence and were sitting back on their heels, faces turned up. Oliver looked down at the presents at his feet, and then at Constance, and lastly, cautiously, at Elizabeth. "Had we better just — change?"

"I suppose so." Her voice sounded harsh and a little desperate. "Go ahead, why don't you?"

She reached the sanctuary of the kitchen; aimlessly, because she was there, she began to heat the coffee again. What a fool she had been to think that Christmas would go un-marked. And what a twisted, what an utterly malicious thing for someone to do — to scram-ble the cards on the presents she had wrapped and put away with such care. No damage, no violence. Just one more thing to bring that baffled look to Oliver's eyes, one more small irrelevance to make her seem irresponsible. To let her know that she was hated.

Oliver found her there, staring fiercely and blindly ahead of her. He closed the door be-hind him, and said quietly, "Take it easy. We're all straightened out now, and no harm done. Come and open your things."

"In a minute." Elizabeth turned her back and focused on the percolator with difficulty, humiliated beyond measure that she should have this defeating impulse to cry merely be-cause Oliver was there. The impulse passed, and she said almost conversationally, "That mix-up was deliberate, you know. I did every card along with the present it went on, just so nothing like this would happen."

Behind her, Oliver was silent. When she turned he said quickly, "You know the old thing about the best-laid plans. But come on —"

"Wait," said Elizabeth; because it was Christmas, she went on hoping in spite of Oliver's eyes. "The cards were all in order when I put the presents in the corner cabinet, Oliver. I know that as well as I know I'm standing here. Whatever happened to them happened after I put them away."

"The cards weren't attached," Oliver pointed out. "Maybe they slithered around —"

". . . And slithered back on to other packages, like the well-trained cards they are?" said Elizabeth with scorn.

There was a flat, uncompromising silence. "Look here," said Oliver, calmly, reasonably. "Are you suggesting that someone deliberately changed them around? I know it's early for me to be up, but — what's the point?"

"This," said Elizabeth, facing him suddenly, "just this. So that you won't believe me and we can stand here like this, not liking each other very much. It's foolproof, isn't it, Oliver? It happens every time."

"Elizabeth —"

131

"Jeep's crying," she said unsteadily. "Go and see what's the matter, can't you?"

Ten minutes later she was back in the living-room with Oliver and Constance, opening her presents, thanking them both. Oliver had a new watchfulness, and she had to endure her cousin's grey unwinking gaze. She tried on the wide tailored white-gold bracelet from Oliver and rubbed Constance's frozen cologne on her wrists and pretended pleasure. Underneath, her anger and shock pounded as steadily as her pulse.

How could they both believe — as they obviously did — that she had mixed up their presents through carelessness? You could only do a thing like that if you were hopelessly drunk, or under the influence of —

*Oh!* thought Elizabeth, cold and aware.

The six missing sleeping pills. Suppose, for instance, that she had come back, tired and nervous, from a shopping trip; suppose she had taken one or even two of the soothing little things and lain down to sleep. Suppose she had not been able to sleep, in spite of the comfortable haze, and had got up to wrap presents instead. . . .

Was that it, was that to be the explanation?

Elizabeth was suddenly and furiously angry. To be at the mercy of hidden manipulation, to have her husband and her cousin go along with it so blindly — it was the only excuse she could find, later, for what she did next.

Maire was piling her tiny dishes absorbedly on the floor, chanting the ingredients of a pie. "Some mustard and some sugar and some salt and some apple sauce and some Dutch Cleanser, that will be a lovely pie."

"Lovely indeed," said Elizabeth. "Shall we ask the oun to dinner, maybe?"

It was as though she had released a spring. Maire dropped the dishes with a clatter and went plummeting into her lap; after one wild glance around her and a gasped "Oun in the house?" she buried her face in Elizabeth's throat.

What should have been triumph turned instead to shame and a deep worry over the child's violently pounding heart. Elizabeth stroked the pink-gold curls, hating herself, and said, "It's all right, darling, there's no oun. There's nothing here to hurt you, Maire, you know we'd never let anything hurt you. . . ."

Maire had seen something outside the house, then. And was terrified of its getting in.

She lifted her head above Maire's, and saw Constance's concerned face and Oliver's frown. Oliver said slowly, "I see what you mean. Noreen will be back tonight, let's not forget to ask her."

But Noreen wasn't back that night, or the next day. And Elizabeth, who had thought she was taxed to capacity, began to know a new and sharper fear.

# 11

The snow began at a little before three o'clock on the day after Christmas. It was gentle and tentative at first, a faint starring against the down-drawn light. By three-thirty the afternoon was white and whirling with it, and Elizabeth, watching at the living-room windows, found that it gave an edge to her growing uneasiness.

She had wondered last night at Noreen's non-appearance; she had been mildly annoyed that morning. When the telephone call an hour ago had turned out to be Oliver, asking if she had heard from the girl, she realized the extent of her worry.

But nothing could have happened to Noreen. It was nonsense to connect her absence with Maire's sudden terror, with the ghostly, ringing 'Oun'.

Behind her, on the floor, Maire said interestedly, "What's that?" and Elizabeth turned to watch Jeep scribbling intently on a sheet of paper.

"Bear," said Jeep tersely.

"Where's his head?"

The pencil never faltered. "Got no head," Jeep said in a tone precluding further discussion, and the telephone rang.

It was Lucy Brent, asking her in mock-tragic tones to come over and see the puppy Steven had given her for Christmas. "It looks like an overgrown mouse — and oh, God, *stop* that — it isn't liking what I gave it for breakfast. Come over and help me bear this, will you?"

"I can't. Constance is out and," Elizabeth said, peculiarly reluctant, "Noreen isn't back."

"Oh, but I thought she . . . well, well," said Lucy with a kind of reviving sparkle. "I've got the car today — do you suppose I could shut this creature into the bathroom with some newspaper and come over there? Does one do that with a month-old puppy?"

She arrived three-quarters of an hour later, just after Elizabeth had installed the children with a basket of blocks on the dining-room floor. She entered like a commando, looking piercingly all around her as though Noreen might be concealing herself behind a chair, challenging Elizabeth at once. "Of all days to be left to your own resources — but then you're entirely too easygoing with servants.

136

Have you heard from her at all?"

"No. I'm quite worried, as a matter of fact."

"Worried?" Lucy produced her lorgnette and stared. "My good girl, why? She'll come back when she's ready, when she's got over Christmas — with a dying uncle or an ailing niece to account for all this. They always do."

Elizabeth listened to the crisp dismissing voice and looked at Lucy's haggard, faintly haughty assurance, and thought about Noreen's huge frightened eyes. She felt her annoyance bobbing up like a cork, and she made no effort at all to restrain it. She said, "Lucy, be fair. You don't like the girl, you never have. If you have any reason to distrust her, or if you know something about her that I don't, I wish you'd tell me."

In the startled second of silence that followed, Maire aimed a block expertly at Jeep's head, and there was an instant storm of tears. Elizabeth lifted him soothingly to her lap and informed Maire that if there was any more throwing of blocks she would confiscate them at once; Jeep went back to the dining-room and said furiously, "Mama says you are a bad, bad gel."

And Lucy had had time to recover herself, to look hurt and surprised. "I didn't mean to upset you, Elizabeth — heavens, I hardly

137

know the girl. It's just that an absence after Christmas does look rather like head-holding."

"If it were that," said Elizabeth, "and it's very difficult to believe that it is when you know her, she'd call me — with an excuse, I admit, but she'd call."

Lucy shrugged. Elizabeth thought, watching her, She does know something about Noreen, or thinks she does. Is that why they're so hostile to each other?

And then, because it was never very far from her mind, she thought about the Hotel Savoia, and it stung across her consciousness like an electric current: Is it possible that Noreen knows something about Lucy?

Lucy was prepared to retreat; she said mildly, "Well, the fact remains that she isn't here and hasn't called you. She'd be rather a handful to kidnap. What's your explanation?"

"I don't know." She was taken up, for the moment, with the memory of Noreen's eyes meeting Lucy's that day on the stairs, level, equal, unafraid. *Recognizing?* She said again, slowly, "I don't know. . . ."

Lucy changed the subject briskly. "She'll turn up. It's a nuisance for you, that's all, stopping your work dead. . . . Have a nice Christmas?" She had put away the lorgnette, and her eyes looked bright and candidly in-

138

quiring. Lucy had known where Elizabeth's presents were stowed, had stood at the door of the cabinet one day, saying ruefully, "Aren't you lucky, you're all done. . . ."

"Very nice." Careful; she would never get anywhere if she couldn't seem as casual as whoever it was who hated her. "Did you?"

"Well, of course, a puppy —" Lucy smiled oddly. "You know, I think it's symbolic on Steven's part. We're to have the patter of four little feet instead of two, and something to tie Lucy down. It's rather sweet in a way, don't you think?"

Her eyes were bitter. Elizabeth felt embarrassed and unwilling, as though she were looking at a part of Lucy that was inadvertently showing. She said crisply, "Steven thought you'd like a dog and he bought one. As a matter of fact, I'd like one myself for the children, and for when Oliver's away."

Lucy stood up, changed and laughing. "Elizabeth dear, if there's one thing I envy you it's your nice sensible head."

"Thank you," said Elizabeth equably. "I'd do anything for your good walking ankles. Do you have to go? It's not quite four-thirty."

"I know." Lucy was moving toward the door, fastening the hood of her black raincoat. "But Steven's coming home early, or at least his office said he'd left for the day when I called. Do let me know if I can babysit for you, or if you hear anything about —"

It was unfortunate that Steven Brent chose exactly that moment to execute a light triple tap at the door.

". . . Tuesday, if you're free for lunch," Steven was saying, five minutes later. "Crale's been wanting to meet you for some time."

Lucy's car, pulled into the drive where Steven hadn't seen it, had driven away in the snowy half-dark almost at once. He had been startled at the sight of his wife; Lucy, after a single brilliant glance at Elizabeth, was casual and — curt. She wouldn't dream of interrupting them; business was business, wasn't it, even under such pleasant circumstances?

"Tuesday's all right," Elizabeth said.

She was still bewildered and a little angry; she didn't like bearing the brunt of Lucy's coolness, or the knowledge that Steven could have said all this over the phone without embarrassing everyone concerned. It made a situation that couldn't have happened six months ago. It had happened now, and even though it was small and ridiculous it was another reminder of how wrong everything was.

Constance had marshalled the children into the kitchen and was preparing their supper. Snow slid softly against the black window-panes of the porch, and Elizabeth, watching it, wondered uneasily about Noreen. Lucy had dismissed the girl's disappearance briskly, tolerantly — but it wasn't as simple as that. In the two months of her stay at the house, Noreen had shown herself as reliable as bread and butter, and almost over-conscientious.

'Oun', screamed Maire in memory, and Lucy's echoed voice said, 'Rather a handful to kidnap'. And here was the night and the snow and the complete lack of communication. . . . Elizabeth stirred. She had the address where Noreen spent the night once a week with another girl. If she hadn't heard by morning . . .

"Elizabeth," said Steven with nervous explosiveness, and she came back with a jolt to the porch and the papers he had flung down with unaccustomed violence. "Do you think Lucy's happy?"

It was the last thing she had expected him to say; it was, at the moment, the last thing she wanted to hear. She looked carefully at Steven, and he was serious, his face worried out of its usual shy calm, his fingers tapping unevenly at the table-top. Heaven only knew what it had taken to make him say this, even to someone he knew and trusted. She said cautiously, "I don't know, Steven — I've always thought so," and finished it out silently

141

and unavoidably in her own mind: But then I am not an authority, as I always thought Oliver was happy too.

She looked at Steven again, and he looked confused and unanswered. She said, "Why? I mean, are you worried about her health, or —"

"No. It isn't anything like that, it . . ." Steven paused, staring down at his linked fingers, before he glanced up again and said uneasily, "I realize it's only a symptom, but — this obsession with bridge. Lucy's got so that she lives for it. It isn't natural, and furthermore —"

He stopped himself in time; he didn't say, except by implication, "We can't afford it." Elizabeth, startled and newly aware, looked back at Lucy's increased sharpness, Lucy borrowing fifty dollars, Lucy bitter about the puppy . . . and what else might Lucy have shown Steven? Elizabeth was suddenly and immensely weary; she thought, I can fight this for myself, but not for Steven.

Rebellion must have shown in her face, because Steven, pacing, turned and said half-apologetically, "It's not a question people ask, I know. It's just that . . . women tell other women things."

"Some women," Elizabeth amended, lightly and firmly.

The snow had increased its velvet swing; outside the porch windows, under the apple tree, the ground was alive with luminous sloping shadows. Steven said suddenly and surprisingly, "You've had enough to cope with, haven't you, without this?"

Elizabeth looked wordlessly startled, and he said, "Sorry — am I speaking out of turn? I thought, the other night when Maire cried out like that —"

She almost told him then. His face was sober and his eyes quietly curious, and she could have got it said without the tears and trembling with which she had told Oliver. And Steven, she knew instinctively, would believe her. But, distantly, a car went slushing by, and she remembered the lonely tail-light of the Brents' old Ford dying into the dusk. She would have liked to pin down Steven's impression that Maire had seen something to frighten her here, among them — but she was firmly determined not to discuss Lucy with him, or to be the cause of delaying him an instant longer.

She stood up, and said without answering anything directly, "Everybody hits a low point some time or other. As a matter of fact, it sounds as though Constance is hitting one right now in the kitchen — I'd better take over."

At the door Steven said casually, "Tuesday for lunch, then — I'll call you about the time.

Christmas go off all right?"

"Beautifully, thanks. . . ." Closing the door behind him, standing for an instant at one of the flanking windows to watch the white and drowning snow, Elizabeth found that her mouth was still stiff from smiling. Steven turned at the hedge to wave, and she lifted a hand. All at once the glass and the distant figure and her own gesture sharpened and became the ingredients of another scene.

The face in Noreen's window, the lazily upraised hand. The drench of perfume said that the intruder had been a woman, but the face itself, looked at abstractly, was not nearly so definite. At that distance, sharply wrong in its surroundings, it could have been a woman's . . . or a man's.

Elizabeth had the children on their way to bed when Maire's terror returned.

She had been chattering about giving her baby a bath. At the foot of the stairs, without warning, she gave her dreadful clear cry and hurled herself wildly against Elizabeth.

Jeep, clutching his bedtime armful of trucks, stopped in bewilderment. In the living-room, Constance came startledly to her feet, saying, "Good heavens, what is it?" Elizabeth ignored both of them. She disentangled Maire very gently from her skirts and sat down on the bottom step of the stairs. She made her voice as businesslike as she could, because the commotion along her nerves told her that whatever had frightened Maire was the dark and secret core of her own pursuing evil.

She said, "Now look here, Maire, what's this all about? Where is this — oun?"

Even said like that, crisply and rebukingly, it carried its own small echoes. Elizabeth had a moment of pure unreason, as though something unknown might be there very near them, horribly eager for the summoning. *Nonsense.* She stopped holding her breath; she watched Maire's eyes, to which vision had slowly returned.

Maire turned her head, fearfully, pressing closer to Elizabeth. She was staring over her shoulder, and Elizabeth followed the wide watchful gaze to the paned glass inner door, the small space between that and the front door itself. Nothing there but shadows and a few bright reflections. . . . "See?" said Elizabeth, ashamed of her own relief. "There's nothing there at all, silly."

Maire gave her a dubious look. She was quiet again but still tense. She repeated slowly and wonderingly, "Nothing there. Oun's all gone," and took her hands out of Elizabeth's and walked sidlingly into the living-room. Elizabeth watched her, Constance stared as though mesmerized; Jeep said, wriggling, "What Maire *doing*, Mama?"

Maire seemed unconscious of all of them. She went the length of the room with that odd, wary, stiff-legged gait, keeping well away from the windows, eyeing the porch door with particular care. Constance turned her head in fascinated silence. Elizabeth stared everywhere Maire did, and thought, her heart beating hard, Something's been at one of the windows.

Because it was glass, any and every glass surface, that Maire was ready to shy at.

But she was, at not-quite-four, quick and self-possessed and almost dangerously without fear. Over-imaginative, possibly, but well aware of the dividing line between fact and her own sportive fancy. And she knew by name everyone and everything that concerned her in the immediate world of the house.

What was it that could leave an observing and articulate child with nothing but a wild crying syllable to describe it?

"I still think," said Oliver, peering concentratedly at the hub on Jeep's tricycle, "that you're getting wound up over nothing. Everybody takes an illegal day off now and then, and Noreen's been pretty good about that so far. Of course, the day after Christmas isn't the most tactful time to . . . The cotter pin's gone off this."

Constance rose and went silently out of the room. Elizabeth stared out at the falling snow, at white-iced cedar branches trembling close to the glass. She couldn't have explained her own feeling of foreboding, her conviction that this was not an ordinary, inconvenient absence — not even, perhaps, a willing one. She said in a muffled voice, "Suppose something's happened to her?"

"You mean the North Shore white-slave ring?" Oliver appeared to consider this solemnly before he bent to the tricycle again. "Got a tweezers?"

Elizabeth's irritation escaped. "I wish you'd put that damned thing down and help me think what to do."

Oliver put the tricycle on its side, dropping his own patience at the same time. "All right — I don't see, frankly, what there is to do."

Constance came back again and handed him a bowl full of small miscellaneous objects collected from around the house, said murmuringly, "Would it be in there?" and sat down again. Elizabeth said, "I could call the police."

"They don't send bloodhounds out after every missing nursemaid — particularly over the holidays." Oliver looked at her, and shrugged. "Well, where did she go for Christmas?"

"To an aunt and uncle in Arlington. But it's a two-family house and the phone isn't in their name. Besides, she was coming back early to spend a few hours with the girl she used to room with here in town."

Constance was frowning at her hands. She said unexpectedly, "I quite agree, Elizabeth. If she were sick, or something had come up in the family, she's the kind of girl who'd get in touch with you. And she's so very young and — gullible that it does make you feel responsible."

Oliver looked moody at the joining of forces. "Well then, why don't you go see the other girl — do you know her name?"

"Rosemary Teale — I think it was Rosemary. In Pinckney Court, which I suppose I could find." Useless, again, to try and define for either of them her own faint but growing dread, her feeling that Noreen and the children stood together in jeopardy, and for the same reason. People didn't bother to conceal things from children or, often, from young, inexperienced, rarely seen-or-spoken-to maids.

The difference was that children could not tell. Maire screamed at reflections in glass, and Noreen was missing.

Rosemary Teale, Pinckney Court . . . "I'll go tomorrow," said Elizabeth.

But, as it turned out, she didn't have to.

# 12

Rosemary Teale, silhouetted in navy blue against the icy blinding world of snow, was like a symbol of safety.

She was a short sturdy girl, perhaps a year or two older than Elizabeth, with an alert squarish face. Her hair was brief and brown and shiny, her voice had a pleasant little-boy hoarseness. She introduced herself crisply when Elizabeth opened the door in answer to the knocker at ten o'clock that morning.

"You're Mrs. March, aren't you? You don't know me, but I'm a friend of Noreen Delaney's — Rosemary Teale. I wonder if I could —"

She stopped, smiling. Elizabeth turned instinctively and saw Maire peering through the banisters as pink and naked as an infant in arms. She said hastily, "Come in, and excuse me a minute, will you, while I get some clothes on my daughter?"

She carried her sense of reassurance upstairs, and held on to it while she struggled

Maire into a dress, located a missing shoe, and separated Jeep from a quiet study of the electric clock in her bedroom. When they were established with old magazines in their own room and she went downstairs again, the reassurance was torn away without preamble. Rosemary Teale, solid and ski-suited in front of the white brick fireplace, said, "I'm worried about Noreen, Mrs. March. I could have phoned, I suppose, but you always feel better if you see people. Have you heard from her at all?"

"No. In fact," said Elizabeth, "I was on the brink of coming to see you. Sit down, won't you, Miss Teale?"

Rosemary Teale sat down. She lighted a cigarette with a concentration of straight dark brows and said in that low, likeably rough voice, "The thing is this. Jill and I — the three of us used to room together — were giving a party on Christmas afternoon. Noreen doesn't drink, but I know she was looking forward to coming — she'd had a dress of Jill's altered to fit her and she said she'd certainly be there. We missed her at the party, and then when I called here and found she hadn't come back, I began to worry."

Constance must have taken the call, and forgotten to tell her. Elizabeth looked at the girl in the wing chair and wondered for the

151

first time how much Rosemary Teale had been told about the March household. The silences, the hostilities, the small inexplicable happenings. She felt her way, cautiously. "It's seemed to me lately that Noreen's been rather worried herself."

"I'm sure of it," said Rosemary Teale with an instant air of relief. "Funny you should say that, because only the other night I said to Jill —"

What she had said to Jill boiled down disappointingly to what Elizabeth had observed for herself: a vague depression on Noreen's part, a haunted air, a thorough retreat into silence. "Except about Maire," said Rosemary Teale. "She's very fond of your little boy — Jeep, is it? — but she worships Maire."

Elizabeth listened and felt herself grow tighter. She said suddenly, interrupting, "Have you her aunt's address in Arlington? If I can get away I'll go there this afternoon."

Yancy Street, Hertford, Lincoln . . . Sycamore. Elizabeth made a right turn and drove slowly down Sycamore Street. It had sounded like a winding and shady road; it stretched endlessly before her, broad, arrow-straight, naked in the thin windy light. The frame houses that lined it solidly on either side seemed at first glance to be a uniform mustard-colour, with curly fret-work porches and a few steep concrete steps going up.

Elizabeth found a parking place three blocks beyond the one she wanted and began to walk back. The houses weren't all that broiled yellow; here and there a two-family building reared a bottle-green head. She passed a kerchiefed woman sweeping snow from a porch, a pink-lipped young man who gave her an inviting smile, a group of small boys with snowballs whom she circled with trepidation. And then she was at No. 203, her heart going at a ridiculous pace.

No. 203 was dressed in peeling mustard, its window-frames brown, the windows themselves curtained in straight-hanging white lace. Elizabeth mounted a double flight of concrete steps and walked to the front door, her heels echoing on the wooden porch. She knocked, and gave her attention to a row of flower-pots just visible through curtains at her left.

She told herself resolutely that the door would not open on tragedy.

Behind her in the street the children shouted dimly. Icicles on the porch roof dwindled with lazy wet little sounds. The painted dark-yellow panels of the door were suddenly snatched from in front of Elizabeth's eyes and she found herself staring at a face instead. The face said instantly, "Well, what is it?"

His voice was soft and high, ludicrous issuing from the thick bold reddish face. Even his glasses were bold, the lenses so thick and curved that behind them his eyes were a huge fierce concentration of brown. He was a big man, not tall, with a look of solid, quick-moving power. Not Ambrose Miller, Elizabeth decided in a flicker, not anybody's uncle.

She lifted her chin a little in the face of the steady, spectacled stare. "I'm looking for Mr. or Mrs. Ambrose Miller. Can you tell me if either of them is in?"

"The Millers?" Again the soft voice, again the scrutiny, calm, taking its time over her scarf, her coat, her booted ankles, rising without hurry to her face. "They live upstairs, but Mr. Miller had a bad spell over Christmas. They don't see people just now."

It was like the door of the room in the Hotel Savoia, closing on what she wanted to know. Elizabeth said urgently, "Mrs. Miller, then? It's quite important — it's about their niece. I'm a friend of hers. I think if they knew that they might —"

The man had stepped back reluctantly, and they were standing in a small dusky hall floored in linoleum. There was a brown plush settee, a glass-fronted whatnot, a flight of

154

stairs at the back. Over everything, a faint compound of dust and horsehair and camphor.

"Niece?" said the man dubiously, eyeing Elizabeth. "Young kid — nineteen, twenty?"

"Yes."

"Dark brown hair, kind of big eyes?"

"Yes, that's the one."

"Well, she isn't here. If she's got any sense she won't come back for a while, either, after the way she took off when Miller's arthritis kicked up. The aunt made a hassle over that, I can tell you, because it was the day after Christmas and — Say." The man craned up the stairs, cautiously, and then back at Elizabeth. "You wouldn't be the one who called for her, would you?"

Called for her . . . Elizabeth's palms went damp inside her gloves while Jagoe — he introduced himself at last — continued, with relish.

Ambrose Miller had had an especially bad turn — there was a heart complication — on Christmas afternoon, and the doctor was sent for. Mrs. Miller had pleaded with her niece to stay at least until the following morning, as there was a great deal to be done for the sick man, and portions of this had floated down to Jagoe.

The aunt: "Don't you feel you owe your

uncle and me at least this much?" Noreen: "Oh, I wouldn't leave until I knew he was better. It wasn't the party I was thinking about, but I'll have to phone the people I work for. They're expecting me tonight."

The aunt again: "I'll call them from the drug store. After all, it's your own flesh and blood. . . ."

"But she didn't call," said Elizabeth involuntarily.

Jagoe gave her a shrewd sidelong glance. "She wouldn't, if it was over a nickel." He said that he had missed the crux of the matter, but that Mrs. Miller had poured it tearfully into his ears: how, while he was out the following morning, the front door bell rang and Noreen was sent to answer it. How, almost instantly, Noreen returned to the Miller apartment and without a word to anyone packed her overnight bag and, deaf to the entreaties of her aunt, walked down the stairs again and out of the house.

Mrs. Miller had slipped down at noon today to use the phone for the grocery order, and informed Jagoe bitterly that her niece hadn't even bothered to call and inquire after her uncle.

The distorted brown eyes were watching her with sharp curiosity and a kind of malicious interest. Elizabeth rose stiffly from the plush settee. No one had dropped a glove, or a match folder, or a distinctive cigarette end in this twilit little half-room. There was nothing here at all but what must have been here for years — the darkly shining glass of the whatnot, the starveling settee, the uncarpeted stairs rising into dimness.

No point in pursuing the resentful Mrs. Miller, thought Elizabeth, out in the air again. Noreen's visitor would have made very sure of that. Bound her to silence when she returned to the Millers' for her bag, using a threat or —

Very suddenly, and as though she were seated beside Elizabeth in the moving car, Rosemary Teale said again, "Noreen worships Maire."

The car jumped, the speedometer needle began, steadily, to rise.

"Everything all right?" repeated Constance. She looked tired and flushed and a little annoyed. "Why, of course, we got along very well. Didn't we, children?"

"Aunt Constance broke a cup," announced Maire; from the excitement in her face she had been saving these tidings for some time. Constance gave her a severe glance. "Yes, I did, Miss — because your brother was about to knock over a lamp. Jeep, tell your mother

157

how naughty you were."

That, thought Elizabeth, was rather a lot to ask of a small boy. She said, "You didn't mean it, did you, Jeep?" and without chancing a reply swept them off to the kitchen for bread and butter and milk. When moderate calm had descended over the table she went back to the living-room to find Constance waiting.

Her cousin held a small round wicker basket on her lap and was sorting through it in an abstracted way. Elizabeth knew without asking that Constance was still searching for the cotter pin from Jeep's tricycle; she would continue searching for it, mildly and undeflectably, long after it had been replaced. It was probably a virtue, Elizabeth thought, but it could also be a very great bore indeed, and she herself always kept her lips firmly closed about a missing glove or lipstick or earring.

Constance glanced up expectantly. "Well? Sit down, Elizabeth, you must be tired — did you find out anything?"

"Nothing that helps much," Elizabeth said, and told her. Impossible not to remember, as she did so, that Constance had left the house early yesterday morning, shortly after Oliver, to exchange his Christmas gloves, which she had bought at a department store in Lynn.

She hadn't come back until a little before noon . . .

"How — peculiar," Constance was saying slowly. She had stopped probing in the basket and was staring thoughtfully ahead of her. "You know, Elizabeth — of course, it isn't really any of my affair, and I wouldn't for worlds go against Oliver's wishes — it does seem to me time you did something. I see Oliver's point about the police, but under the circumstances —"

Elizabeth's gaze swung up from her cigarette. Constance said after the barest of pauses, ". . . as she is in your employ, and rather young to be on her own like this, I think you'd be amply justified in letting the police know."

"You're right, of course," Elizabeth said, and glanced unnecessarily at the clock. "I'll — they may want to come here, so I think I'll wait until the children are in bed."

Foolish, even dangerous, to postpone the deadline.

And utterly impossible to explain her own last-minute reluctance, as though she walked on the edge of a precipice and any positive action on her part would be the equivalent of the push that would send her plunging.

"Do," said Constance soothingly, in her other existence. "Now, isn't this annoying. I *know* I picked up that cotter pin . . ."

159

The deadline narrowed. Jane Perrin phoned to say that her sister was up from Baltimore, and would Elizabeth and her cousin and Oliver come and meet her over highballs that evening? Elizabeth said that they would love to but were sitterless, and went away from the phone more edgy than she had been before its beckoning ring.

Jeep slipped on one of his beloved trucks and cut his lip with a tooth; Maire said pleasedly, "Can I see the bleed?" Elizabeth poached eggs and stirred cocoa and cut toast into slender fingers, and kept seeing the clock, and Oliver's stormy face when she told him she had called the police.

With darkness, the melting snow had frozen. The night was full of tiny sliding reflections, the lilacs thrust against the pantry window, bony and silver. Maire and Jeep begged to be excused their bath so that they could sit under the lighted Christmas tree, and Elizabeth said yes and went back to the dishes.

The hot water rushed and rinsed; the lilacs tapped at the black panes. Elizabeth turned off the faucet once to make sure that it was only the lilacs; she was suddenly and pricklingly nervous. Which was ridiculous, of course, because Constance and the children were only two rooms away.

You're all alone with Constance, observed her mind.

And: Oliver will be late tonight, because of the icy roads.

She turned sharply and reached for a dish towel, and her unsteady fingers sent a cup smashing to the floor.

She thought, picking up the pieces, that if the beginning of fear had been like a virus, then this was the final, the killing stage, when a random and foolish thought could affect her nerves like a pounce in the dark.

She had forgotten the spoons, and the cocoa pot. She carried them to the sink and washed them, making herself move briskly, making more noise than she had to in order to defy the golden kitchen silence, the black windows, the rattling night.

Because of that, she didn't hear the knock in time. What she did hear was the faint creak of metal as someone tried the knob of the back door. Had it been entirely the lilacs, then? Who — ?

Elizabeth was suddenly so terrified that she dropped the dish towel and stood still, one wrist gripped tightly in her other hand. She could feel the receding hollowness in her chest where fear had hit her like a physical impact, and then desperation carried her out into the middle of the kitchen, where she stood frozenly and faced the back door.

It opened, hesitantly, and Noreen Delaney came in.

And Elizabeth stared, shocked into silence.

# 13

Noreen's face, inside the blue figured folds of her kerchief, was white and incredibly worn. The blue-brown shadows under her eyes had deepened until they looked carven, the eyelids themselves were swollen and grey. The small pale mouth was down-drawn and rigid, as though only the most desperate of efforts were keeping it steady.

Relief, and even any kind of normal greeting, fled from Elizabeth for the long suspended moment in which Noreen stared back across the kitchen at her, eyes empty of everything but fatigue. This was the girl who had left the house three days ago, flushed and smiling. . . .

She found her tongue at last and said very gently, "What's the matter, Noreen?" and Noreen answered her barely above a whisper.

"Do you still want me to work for you, Mrs. March?"

"Of course," said Elizabeth, deliberately crisp. "Whatever it is can wait until you've had some hot tea. I'll put water on. . . ."

So there was a small cup-and-saucer interval in which Noreen could steady herself, and Elizabeth could try to quiet her own leaping urgency. Instinct told her to go very carefully indeed, now that the prize was within her grasp, because Noreen Delaney must be coaxed and not pulled out of her defensive retreat.

She set the tea to steep, listening tautly to the rustle of fabric, the click of a hanger in the small back hall. She jumped when the swing door from the dining-room opened and Maire put her head inquisitively in.

"Out," said Elizabeth firmly.

"Who came in?" asked Maire, equally firm.

"The wind. Back to your records, it's nearly bedtime."

Maire vanished. At the stove, Elizabeth poured tea and was aware out of the corner of her eye that Noreen had emerged into the kitchen again and was standing uncertainly beside the table. She carried the cups over and managed to set them down without a quiver; she sat down herself with an air of briskness, and after a second or two Noreen murmured her thanks and took the opposite chair.

In the living-room, Constance was evidently aware of the situation; the musical nursery rhymes had reached a strenuous pitch. Elizabeth heard that, and the imperative questions lined up in her own mind. She waited, edged and expectant, while Noreen met her eyes and then bent her head and stirred her tea. When nothing happened at all after that, when the silence grew harder to break with every passing second, Elizabeth looked hard at the slanted-down face across the table and said, "Something happened over Christmas, didn't it, Noreen?"

"Yes." It was blurred and almost inaudible, and the girl's eyes didn't lift, but still it was a start.

Elizabeth gathered her firmness. "Hadn't you better tell me about it? If there's anything at all we can do" — the irony of that struck at her even as she said it — "we'd be only too glad to." She caught the answer to that before it came, because there was so very much at stake. Everything, in fact, depended on this young and frightened girl, inarticulate to begin with, now frozen into muteness. She said, "People can help, sometimes, even when you think they can't."

Noreen looked up then. She said, "There's nothing you can do," in a voice of dead quiet.

Does she know, thought Elizabeth in sudden fury, does she *know* what a knell that is? Half of her went out in pity to the beaten-

165

looking girl opposite her; the other half was tigerish, defending everything she loved, seeing a possible ally turning timidly away.

The anger prevailed. She set her cup down with care and said, watching her words as though they were printed on paper, "Look here, Noreen. What you do with your own time isn't any concern of mine. I do think that in this instance, for my own peace of mind, I'm entitled to some sort of explanation. In the first place, you look as though you ought to be in bed — and if you've been ill, or had any kind of . . . shock — that's where you'd better go. Is that it, is that the trouble?"

Silence for a moment, and then the echo of the front door closing. That would be Oliver, Elizabeth thought bleakly, just when she would have wished him miles away.

Noreen was crying soundlessly, her mouth shaking, her lids lowered. The tears slipped down her pale cheeks, and Elizabeth watched them and hardened herself. You could fight fire with fire, but you couldn't turn timidity on itself.

She said, "Is it something in this house that's kept you away, Noreen?"

The girl shook her head; she didn't look at Elizabeth. Was it impatience at her own tears, an effort at control? Or an answer, to be reassured by?

Elizabeth didn't find out, because the door opened and Oliver came in, with the children noisily in his wake. The kitchen was all at once in turmoil and that, for the time being, was the end of it.

The children were pleased to see Noreen, and Elizabeth watching with a focus that had narrowed to obscure everything else, watched the girl's arms go tightly around Maire at the first opportunity.

Had Noreen's absence had anything to do with a threat to the child — was Maire, who had been shaken to her centre by what she called 'the oun', to become a target too?

It was an intolerable thought. Elizabeth thrust it back with an effort and concentrated on the reactions instead.

Oliver said flatly, "I think you're being hard on the girl. She's of age — suppose she's been going around with some guy who's been shipped out to Korea, or just out, period, and she's embarrassed to tell you she spent every available minute with him?"

Constance said thoughtfully, "I had a few words with her, Elizabeth, and I've a notion it's family trouble. Oh, not the uncle or aunt, but perhaps some disreputable relative she won't admit to but was called upon to help. People do have relatives they hide,

167

and if there'd been some sort of scandal, or trouble with the police . . ."

Lucy Brent said airily, the next day, "Not a word about the last moments at the sickbed? Heavens, I misjudged the girl."

It was the airiness, and something under it, that took Elizabeth out that afternoon to see Lucy.

The Brents lived in a house that Elizabeth had always coveted, a shapely old house set under maples with a deliberately prim picket-fenced lawn. The harbour lay below it; behind rose a tumble of grey mossy rocks that ended the park above. At some point in its lifetime the house had been painted a serene smoke-blue that looked like a reflection from the water; Lucy and Steven had added the snowy shutters and the white brick chimney.

Elizabeth, arriving, glanced around her at the charming yellow and white and russet living-room Lucy had contrived out of auctions and cunning. "Where's the puppy?"

"Oh, the shepherd?" said Lucy, casual. "As a matter of fact I — we gave him to the people down the lane. He was a dear little thing, but you know me about the house . . ."

Elizabeth did know, which startled her all the more: Lucy was one of those rare and expert beings about whom order always seemed

168

to appear without effort. She had a sudden flashing vision of Lucy driving off into the snow the afternoon Steven had dropped in without warning; of Lucy iced and angry, walking into the house, looking at the puppy, picking up the telephone . . .

Lucy was looking at her, and saying, "It must be wonderful to have Noreen back and be able to get out again. She still hasn't said?"

Elizabeth shook her head, and told her. She made it short and matter-of-fact: her own visit to the house on Sycamore Street, Noreen's stricken silence. And she watched, and went completely unrewarded. Lucy said reflectively, "She must have gone of her own free will — people don't abduct grown girls in full daylight. Did you get to see the aunt?"

Elizabeth said she hadn't, and Lucy shrugged. "I suppose she'll tell you some day — when she gets around to it."

There was, again, that odd intimation of something known and withheld. Elizabeth didn't pursue it, she had tried that and failed. She sat through another cigarette, and thought that she reminded herself a little of a research chemist who had set cultures to grow, and went the rounds now and then to see what was happening.

A number of people got killed that way,

finding out too late which tube contained the deadly thing.

Elizabeth had said she must go, and was fishing for a glove that had slipped down between the cushion and the arm of the loveseat, before she discovered that Lucy wasn't quite the impeccable housekeeper she had thought. Something else came up with the white pigskin. A twist of metallic purple that had, surely, covered a bon-bon.

She went upstairs early that night, leaving Oliver and Constance in possession of the living-room, because there seemed no further point in presence. They knew she was in another world, their eyes discussed her. There were invisible head-shakings, soundless comments. Elizabeth wondered curiously and a little coldly if this was how you felt when you were getting — peculiar.

Who could hate her enough for this, when she stood in nobody's way? When her life boiled down to the facts that she was a perhaps-happier-than-average wife, the mother of two small children, a writer of very small renown? No fortunes at stake, no momentous secrets, no one she had wronged, or been wronged by. Nothing to single out her existence from any other woman's, except to herself because she loved it.

Unless — and this was openly terrifying —

there were no reason at all. Any more than an avalanche had reason, or a lightning bolt. Someone near her slipping out of control, destroying blindly, purposely, for destruction's sake. . . .

Elizabeth brushed her hair ferociously, trying to deaden the sound of Noreen Delaney's voice saying tonelessly, "There's nothing you can do."

Because if someone were deriving pleasure from tearing flowers and ruining Jeep's birthday, forging her cheques and removing her sleeping pills, turning Christmas morning into a quiet horror, that form of domestic upset would very soon start to grow tame. There would have to be a stronger, sharper excitement. . . .

Oliver came into the bedroom, startling her; she had planned on being in bed, feigning sleep, because that was easiest. He went past her into the bathroom; the shower rushed briefly. Elizabeth smoked a cigarette and waited, and at the appointed moment stepped casually past him. "Water still hot? If it is, I think I'll have a bath."

It took her a long time, afterwards, to forget the moment when she came back into the bedroom, and Oliver looked at her and put down a cigarette, unlighted, and crossed the room to her without saying anything at all.

171

She turned her back swiftly, pretending absorption in a bottle of cologne, but his hands came down on her shoulders, light, wordless, demanding.

"Oh, don't, *don't* —" Panic wrenched her away, turned her suddenly rigid, risking a glance, not daring to glance again at Oliver's dark and angry face.

The electric clock hummed audibly for a moment. Elizabeth stared at the floor and controlled her involuntary trembling; when she looked up at Oliver, still formidably close, his face was expressionless. He said coolly, "Sorry if I frightened you — my error," and walked violently past her to the closet. When he emerged he had a robe slung over his shoulder. He said politely, "I'll be downstairs reading. You won't, I'm sure, wait up," and closed the door behind him.

Elizabeth went to bed and eventually to sleep, her face wet and aching in the solitary dark.

"Pigs can't swim," said Maire suddenly from the back seat.

"Pigs go oink-oink-OINK!"

"And little boys sit quietly on the seat," said Noreen, interrupting Jeep's mounting shout.

Elizabeth put the car around a corner, glanced briefly into the rear-view mirror and smiled. It had been an inspiration to sweep all of them out of the house for a drive; it was like a blowing-away of cobwebs. The children, who had been threatening all morning to push each other down the stairs, were amicable again, reporting the view from their separate windows. Noreen sat between them, her cheeks pink, her eyes bright with pleasure. Every now and then, at something the children said, she would give a soft little spurt of laughter, as though it had been sealed inside her for too long and was beginning to bubble rebelliously out.

Elizabeth thought she understood; she felt her own mood lift as she drove. She took a contrary pleasure in this aimless expedition, as though she had slipped away from some dark and clinging presence, almost as though she had outwitted it. No one had known they were going to do this, and it followed quite simply that nothing could spoil it.

Over the last wooded hill and down to the harbour, where the water rustled greenly about the dock; Elizabeth stopped the car and took out her cigarettes. It was too cold for the children to get out and sit on the wooden benches. Noreen said, "I'll just take them up the end and back, shall I, Mrs. March?" and Elizabeth nodded and watched them go.

So small, really, when you looked at them

as a stranger might. Elizabeth thought back to her conversation with Noreen Delaney that morning. The girl had been clearly mystified by her mention of the 'oun' — and as clearly worried, putting into words what Elizabeth had felt all along. "I hate to see Maire afraid of anything, she's got so much — I guess it's trust. She gets very gossipy in her bath — perhaps if I asked her in a roundabout way tonight?"

Elizabeth put it out of her mind firmly; that, and her own growing, helpless dread belonged to the house and the existence she had managed to shake off for an hour. Noreen and the children approached the car, and she smiled at the three of them coming back identically rosy, and turned the car reluctantly for home.

It was on the way back that chance entered the quiet deadly battle for the first time. Elizabeth was threading through the streets of the town when a small rattling sound she had been vaguely aware of for some time turned suddenly into a clatter. It came from the rear of the car. It was something caught and dragging, or —

A policeman solved it for her, motioning her to the curb. Elizabeth rolled her window down and looked up at the stiff weather-reddened face. He was new, she hadn't seen him before. He said with a kind of leisurely disapproval, "How long since you've looked at your rear licence plate?'

"About an hour," Elizabeth said mildly. "I'm sorry, Officer, it seemed all right then."

"Well, it doesn't seem all right now." He was sour and deliberate, bending to squint into the back of the car, returning his stare to Elizabeth. "If I hadn't stopped you, lady, you'd have left that plate in the street."

There followed a brusque lecture on general maintenance. Elizabeth said again that she was sorry and would have it attended to at once, and was surreptitiously shifting gears when the policeman said abruptly, "Are you a resident here?"

"Yes." He *was* new, and ambitious. Elizabeth dipped into her bag for her wallet, unzipped the inner compartment where she kept her driver's licence and thrust her gloved fingers inside a little impatiently.

She took everything out of her wallet, and explored every compartment of her bag, before she was sure that the driver's licence was gone.

# 14

A police sergeant whom Elizabeth knew arrived, and sent her on her way with a wink and a warning. She drove home in a quiet numbness, listening to the children's, "What did the man say, Mama?"; hearing only the confusion in her own mind.

She had last used her driving licence as identification two days before Christmas, when in a flurry of last-minute shopping she wrote a cheque for Constance's doeskin gloves. She remembered very clearly putting the licence, folded small, back into its compartment in her wallet, because the zipper had caught, running up, and the salesgirl had said sympathetically that workmanship wasn't what it used to be. She had managed to get the zipper up at last — and she hadn't had occasion to use the licence since.

So it had been removed deliberately from her wallet.

She didn't tell Oliver. She knew he would not believe in her own certainty, and it had become instinctive with her to avoid issues between them. She applied for a new licence, and when it came, folded it inside the five-dollar bill she always carried in the cylinder attached to her car keys.

New Year's Eve came and went. Constance announced a little stiffly that she had made plans of her own; Elizabeth and Oliver went to a party at the Perrins'. The Brents were there, and approximately twenty other people. Elizabeth wore black that showed a thousand pleats when she stirred, and thought she was doing very well until Jane Perrin said with midnight frankness, "Elizabeth, it's so good to see you, and so wonderful of you to come when anybody can see you're not well."

Hollows about her throat, a restlessness in her hands, a new habit of starting at sudden sounds — all of it showing, in spite of a gaiety donned as carefully as the extravagant black gown.

And Oliver watching her across the room: that, thought Elizabeth, was the worst of all. His eyes examining her as though she were someone else's wife, interesting but not for him. And did she imagine it, or was there a new quality to his constant study that night — a watchfulness, like a man who has brought his hydrophobic wife to a swimming meet?

Was Oliver afraid of what she might do, or say?

He was — and she hadn't known how bitter this could be — her escort, in the severest sense of the word. She had come with him and she would leave with him, and in between, even when he was at her side, there was nothing.

It was on the third day of the new year that Jeep brought her the thing that, like a reagent, began to show her the first dim outlines of the pattern.

She had just come down from the studio, having taken a perilous and on the whole pleasing plunge at a first chapter. Noreen had seen her descending the hill and was assembling the little tea-tray; Elizabeth thanked her, shivering, and carried it into the living-room. That was when Jeep came tiptoeing out of the small front hall, clearly enchanted with some project of his own.

His left hand dangled ingenuously at his side, his right was hidden behind him. His little square face beamed as he said in the challenging tone Elizabeth used over different-coloured lollipops, "Which hand, Mama?"

Elizabeth appeared to meditate and soberly chose the hand behind his back. It would be a penny, or a rubber band, or a block . . . but, this time, it wasn't. It was a strip of shiny, crinkly paper, perhaps an inch and a half wide and four inches long, with the edges of a chartreuse and silver design.

She said, only half looking at it, "Thank you, Jeep, that's what I call handsome. I'd better put it away before I lose it."

Jeep climbed into her chair. His momentous and all-knowing air was gone; he said plaintively, "What is it, Mama?"

"What is it? Oh, a piece of paper, left over from Christmas, maybe . . ."

She really looked at it then, and realized in a puzzled way that it was not gift wrapping, that she had seen it somewhere before very recently and that it had a definite echo in her memory. She knew it as certainly as she had known — why did she think of this? — that the twist of purple foil in Lucy's loveseat was a bon-bon wrapper. She took it gently out of Jeep's toying fingers and examined it more closely.

It was one end of an envelope; she could see the fold and the beginning structure of corners. There was only enough black lettering on the chartreuse part to tantalize: ". . . ue" in flowing script; under that, in small block capitals, ". . . ney."

Elizabeth turned the strip of paper over in her fingers, unable to explain to herself her sudden sharp interest. She had seen this, or something very like it, before, and that was all. Or was it all? Why was she lifting it out of Jeep's reach, why did she feel this remembering tingle?

She said cautiously, "Pretty, isn't it, Jeep? Where did you find it?" and Jeep, all pride again, said kindly, "I show you," and caught her hand.

He led her first to the dining-room and, palpably at a loss, pointed under the radiator. "No, not there," Elizabeth said patiently, and Jeep, anxious not to lose the spot light so gratifyingly focused on him, repudiated the radiator and said with growing confidence, "I show you, Mama."

Elizabeth followed him up the stairs, and looked in a number of unlikely places before she realized that he was merely prolonging the game. Perversely, the silvery scrap gained importance. She was standing in the upper hall, still fingering it, saying, "Jeep dear, try and remember where you found it," when Constance mounted the stairs, her coat over her arm. She said mildly, "I had no idea it was so cold outside . . . are you looking for something, Elizabeth?"

For once, her cousin's unceasing vigilance would probably have helped. Elizabeth knew

180

that even as she closed her fingers over the fragment of paper and said lightly, "No, but we're pretending to, aren't we, Jeep?"

Jeep gave her a betrayed stare. He said injuredly, "Where pretty paper, Mama?" and Elizabeth said firmly, "Maire's calling you, Jeep, better run."

In her own room, she smoothed out the chartreuse and silver strip again and examined it, trying to recapture the casual identification her mind had made once before. Or no, twice, because someone — near her? with her? outside the house, at any rate — had commented on it, and she had looked again and been, it was coming closer now, amused.

If she had seen it outside the house, chances were she had been Christmas shopping . . . but where, and with whom?

In the days after that, Elizabeth found to her astonishment that she could actually work, that it was as though her studio lay outside the perimeter of danger. She bought a hot plate and some instant coffee and a supply of cigarettes, and spent her mornings there, banging at her typewriter with a concentration she'd never felt before, sprawling full-length on the couch to read and try to assess what she'd written, lighting a cigarette with one already burning in the tray beside her, go-

181

ing back to the typewriter to take up again or to scrap what she'd done and rewrite.

She was almost happy, in the studio. She could forget temporarily the shock of her new relationship to Oliver, Maire's terrors, the mystery of Noreen's absence, the possible meaning of the bon-bon wrapper in Lucy Brent's loveseat. If her own life were crumbling around her, she built new ones for other people out of inked ribbon and yellow paper. She was half aware of the uselessness of that even as she took comfort from it, but at least she was doing something with the waiting period.

Because it was just that, a waiting. While someone went on hating her for the everyday things she possessed, and inched closer. There would be a pounce, when the hatred overran itself.

But meanwhile, if in the studio she lived in borrowed freedom, the cobweb waited quietly for her in the house — clinging, reminding, brushed away only to entangle her again. A glance from Oliver could set it quivering, or a word from Constance. A look from Noreen, as though she reflected Maire's panic; a visit from thin, nervous, sharp-eyed Lucy.

It was not a new year at all, it was a deterioration of the old. Nothing happened to punctuate the slow and terrifyingly domestic decay

182

until Saturday of the second week-end in January.

It was a day of curbed violence right from the start; wild drumming winds, thrashing branches, an echoing rain that changed to a sleet like silver pepper at the windows. Oliver awoke holding Elizabeth personally responsible for the weather, and Elizabeth, sharply nervous over the hollow, mocking, here-and-there sounds of the storm, flashed at him.

After breakfast Noreen, measuring the temper of the house, spirited the children away upstairs. Constance announced unexpectedly that she had agreed to take a table at the library tea: "Such a shame, isn't it, that we should have weather like this for it?" So that at a little before eleven o'clock that morning Elizabeth and Oliver had the downstairs part of the house to themselves.

It was as awkward as though they were strangers waiting for a mutual hostess, not liking the look of the party.

Oliver was silent and restless, patrolling rather than walking, stopping abruptly to stare through the drenched panes. Would he like more coffee? No, thank you, he would not. A beer, then? She might have offered him hemlock.

Elizabeth said edgily at last, "If you're so

bent on walking, couldn't you make more progress outside?"

"Thanks, but I feel rotten."

"If you're sick you ought to go to a doctor."

Oliver wheeled; he said explosively, "*I* ought to go to a doctor?" and there was a flaming silence.

He went on walking, with a pattern of pauses that registered only dimly on Elizabeth's mind, because she was saying in an off-hand voice she would never have thought she could achieve, "You know, we can't go on like this, Oliver. Don't look so astonished — it's time we brought it into the open, don't you think?"

This was what was known as burning your bridges. It wasn't planned, but there came a time when you could take no more. Elizabeth said, forcing herself to be quiet and even, "You think I'm a hysterical idiot, all swallowed up in morbid self-pity over the baby, taking too many sedatives, imagining things. And I think" — damn her voice for starting to shake — "that you're the stair that wasn't there, so that you let me trip and make a fool of myself. I know better now, and I won't make the same mistake any more. No more confiding tears, and," said Elizabeth, steady again, "no more trust. You're interested elsewhere, you —"

The telephone rang, shockingly loud. Oliver was across the room before the second peal had stopped. He lifted the receiver and listened a moment. He said disinterestedly, "Afraid you have the wrong number," and dropped it with a click.

And the pattern of his walk stood out suddenly clear for Elizabeth.

The turn, past the phone. The halt — beside the phone. The waiting for a call, with the inevitable, unwelcome fact of her being there because the storm had kept her from her usual Saturday morning shopping. Because she felt that the knowledge must show, and because she couldn't bear to look at Oliver just then, Elizabeth turned her back abruptly and straightened folds of a striped linen curtain. Behind her, so close that she stiffened, Oliver's voice said tautly, "Elizabeth, you've got to believe me —"

"Do I? Why, I wonder, when you don't believe me?" She slipped past him, head bent, seeing in a blur.

"Elizabeth — where are you going?"

"Anywhere. For a walk." That at least came out steadily enough. But she had to face him again to get her raincoat from the closet — and Oliver was suddenly looking at her as though she were a lamp, or a table; all his consciousness was somewhere else. His gaze,

185

narrow and intent, was seeing someone else — at another telephone, furious at being cut off?

Elizabeth got her raincoat and put it on. Oliver said in a short absent voice, "Don't get soaked," and started up the stairs.

Of course — the extension in their bedroom, put in a week ago. Elizabeth had suddenly wanted it, pleading the possibility of fire, needing to know that there was more than one means of communication in the house. She pulled on her boots now, and listened.

Oliver had gone into their bedroom, but he hadn't closed the door. There was a peculiar halted quiet, as though he were standing there, listening, charting the silence. But the bedroom windows looked over the front lawn. . . .

Rapidly, feeling the pound of her heart, Elizabeth went to the back door, opened it on a violence of wind and sleety rain, slammed it echoingly and waited an instant. Her boots were rubber, and noiseless; she was able to go back to the telephone without a sound, to lift the receiver gently and hear the faint airy wait along the line.

And then Oliver's voice, not absent now, but urgent. A Boston number, and the drawl as it rang. Elizabeth did not apologize to herself; her visit to the Hotel Savoia had killed that kind of sensitivity. She listened, hardly breathing, hearing the sound of Oliver's breath, until there was a rising click and a voice said sleepily, "Hello?"

Male or female? Elizabeth couldn't be sure; it sounded muffled and husky. Whichever it was, Oliver identified it at once. He said, startlingly close to her ear, "What the hell's the idea? I told you not to call me here."

The answering voice was lazy. "I told you to come across."

"For an envelope. Forgetting that?" Elizabeth hardly recognized Oliver's tight and ugly tone. She stared ahead of her, memorizing a strip of banister, a pulse of rainy light at the hall window.

"Forgetting nothing. You had your instructions. If it's too much trouble, I can always get in touch with Mrs. —"

"Damn you to hell!" It was the first time Elizabeth had ever heard it said like an obscenity. This was Oliver, the Oliver she didn't know, that three months' courtship, five years of marriage hadn't even permitted her to see. Different — appallingly so. Dangerous, because of his very control. Was it because he had never been so seriously crossed before?

Elizabeth listened to the silence following Oliver's curse; it was enigmatic. Oliver said roughly, "Okay, let's get it over with. Where — when?" and she put down the receiver as quietly as she could, unable to listen to more, swept by a cold, sick reaction.

She closed the front door carefully behind her. The rain, at any rate, was clean.

She had not been alone in her watching of Oliver at the Savoia. Someone else knew, someone with a voice that held a faint, disguised familiarity, and Oliver was paying blackmail. Angrily, dangerously — but paying it.

Wind and cold and sleet-needled rain were therapy only so long. Elizabeth walked blindly and furiously away from the house, and became gradually aware that she was nearing the town and that she was chilled through. That, and a faint warning mistiness in her head, made her walk past the toy shop, the jeweller's, the police station, to the neon nakedness of the drug store. She found an empty phone booth, she heard herself saying floatily, "This is Mrs. Oliver March. I'm at Corbett's — can I get a cab right away?"

In the drug store proper, a black-coated woman, seal-shaped, said earnestly to a clerk, "But I'm quite sure I bought this same size bottle a month or two ago for two forty-nine, and the other man, the red-haired fellow, charged me two seventy-five."

Her small head wove, peering, doubtless, for the perfidious red-haired fellow. Elizabeth watched in a mist: the clerk murmured and slid away behind a high counter, the seal-shaped woman snapped her purse open and shut in a nervous tattoo and sidled along to another display. It was a bank of hair-dyes, capped by the enormous cardboard head of a blonde.

The bank was chartreuse and silver. Elizabeth walked closer, knowing that this was important, trying to think through the sudden blazing furriness in her brain. She was sick, suddenly and bewilderingly sick; that was why she had waked so raw and shaken. But this *was* important, this chartreuse and silver. She mustn't lose sight of it, because it meant something, it was like a face calling out for identification. It was Jeep, with a hand clenched solemnly behind him. . . .

Elizabeth went directly up to the display. In spite of her wet hands, her faintly dizzy head, the shells of heat that went peeling and pulsating away from her body, she could still be quite sure of what she was seeing, fully aware of its meaning. The fragment of chartreuse and silver Jeep had found became magically whole, on the top of the bank at the right. It said, 'Halo-Hue', and under that, 'Pink Honey'.

And Steven Brent said, in the memory of a chance encounter, "You ought to sue, it's your colour."

She had been amused then, but she wasn't now. She thought in a sudden merciless wave of clarity: The cheques. The driving licence. The hair dye.

Someone else able, at will, to become Elizabeth March.

# 15

Out of the week that slid by, while she recovered from grippe and pleurisy, Elizabeth was able to isolate certain sharp moments that stood up like barbs along the strung strained wire of her fear.

There was the moment when she awoke from a deep flushed sleep to hear her own voice whispering, "Why are you staring at me?" She whispered it to the clear image of Constance's face, bent close and intent just above her own, frighteningly expressionless.

"Staring?" Constance's mild echo came from across the room. When Elizabeth lifted her head, her heart still beating confusedly, she saw that her cousin was standing in the open doorway to the bathroom, a glass in her hand. "You've been asleep nearly an hour," said Constance. "How do you feel?"

"Better . . ." It had been a dream, then. Had to have been, because no one would crouch over a bed like that, just — staring at a sleeping face.

There was the day Lucy Brent came, shedding her sharpness and her lorgnette, warmly concerned. "You poor thing. There's grippe all over town, if that's any consolation. I won't ask how you feel, because I know you're wretched, but I'm just on my way to town and there must be something I can get you. Books? Here, better write me a list . . ."

Noreen Delaney had just set down Elizabeth's lunch tray. Elizabeth watched and wondered over the lift of the girl's eyes to Lucy before she went silently out.

A dream, a glance . . . at times, during that week, Elizabeth felt like a suggestible child at the mercy of a malicious elder. Were Oliver and Constance and Lucy right after all — was she a victim of her own nerves, subconsciously putting off adjustment to the fact of a stillborn child? The odd new peace, the difference in Oliver, the serenity with which the household ran without her argued that she was.

And she might have believed it, if it were not for the envelope of hair-colouring that stood like a montage over every face around her. That was not nerves, but physical fact. Jeep, whose fingers were everywhere, must have torn it from a packet in a woman's purse.

Why, when payment on the cheques had been stopped, would another woman want to

192

assume the name of Elizabeth March?

But payment could not be stopped at hotels, or stores.

Had she an understudy?

The bed that had seemed so blissful became all at once intolerable, in spite of the damp ache of grippe, the stab of pain just under her right shoulder blade. She must have waked a hundred times, out of thought or out of sleep, to a panicky listening for the children.

It didn't help to realize that the logical tools of imposture bore no relation to the romping malice that had gone before: the wrenching apart of the roses, the sickening of the children on Jeep's birthday, the sardonic transposing of her Christmas presents.

Because it was, it must be, the same concentrated brain at work; so honeycombed with hatred of her that it was hardly, by now, a functioning brain at all.

". . . Perhaps tomorrow," said Dr. Malloway, disapprovingly.

Tomorrow turned out to be a day of thaw, blue and windy, with the lawn as soaked and springy as it was in April and the lilacs black and moist and hopeful. Elizabeth put on a housecoat, out of deference to Oliver's reluctance that she get up at all that morning, and a faint touch of rouge, out of deference to herself, because her face looked so starkly white in the bathroom mirror.

Oliver, worried and still angry at himself for having let her go out into the storm on that critical Saturday, said, "Don't go feeling your oats."

"I won't."

"What you'd better do," said Oliver, looking at her earnestly, "is go back to bed and then get up for lunch and go back to bed and so forth."

"I'll see . . ." She felt stumblingly new in this relationship, not knowing how far to trust the warmth, the normalcy.

"Whatever you do," Oliver downed his coffee, looked at his watch and stood, "don't go up to the studio. That's probably where you caught cold in the first place. Is Constance ready, do you think?"

"Whenever you are," said Constance from the doorway. Her arms were laden with rental library books; she over-rode Elizabeth's protests. "Nonsense, it's a beautiful day and the walk back will do me good. And these books really ought to be returned. Is there anything else you'd like me to get you while I'm there?"

Elizabeth said no and watched them drive away, wondering, as she had wondered every morning during the past week, if today were

194

the day of Oliver's appointment with the sleepily vicious voice on the telephone. Or perhaps he had already taken care of that — until the demand for more money should come again.

She was alone in the house. Noreen had taken the children for an after-breakfast walk, clearly doubtful about leaving Elizabeth. She had said in a low voice, for Elizabeth's ears alone, "Are you sure you'll be all right, Mrs. March?" and for an instant, meeting the shadowed eyes, Elizabeth sensed the same recognition she had felt in Maire's room on the night the child cried out. It put them both on an oddly different basis. She said without smiling, "I don't know why I shouldn't be, Noreen — do you?"

The girl's eyelids dropped; Elizabeth, watching, thought she saw a faint rise of colour in the thin face. But when Noreen glanced up again the oddness, the other meanings might have been imagined. She said in a defensive tone, "Mr. March is very anxious that you shouldn't get over-tired on your first day up, and I just thought . . ."

Well, that was all right, thought Elizabeth now, going back to the kitchen for another cup of coffee. And if Oliver had also spoken to Constance, that was all right too, and only normal anxiety. It didn't mean that she was being . . . watched in another sense, and it was foolish to connect it with Oliver's warning her away from the studio.

The swish of her housecoat was loud in the silence. She finished her coffee and wandered idly into the living-room with a cigarette. Gradually a small uneasiness grew, a deepening of the feeling she had had once before: that the walls and chairs and mirrors, hidden from her for a week, held a touch, an imprint, a reflection she would have given almost anything to identify.

Whose?

The cigarette turned suddenly bitter. Elizabeth rose in a rustle and went to the windows, not wanting to let the thought take possession. It was always there in her mind, of course; it was like a lens through which she saw everything else. But if she lingered over it, if she let it grow, it swelled until it occupied her entire brain and there was nothing in her but a black blind fear.

. . . It had almost happened now. Elizabeth, at the window, became slowly aware that she had been curling her fingers in and out of her palms in a quickening, tightening tempo, and that the palms themselves were damp. She flattened them hard against the cold glass; she thought wonderingly, Anyone seeing me now would think . . .

Far down at the end of the road, half-screened by intervening branches, the nose of a black car pulled into view and halted. A man got out of the car, and then a woman. Something about the man's build, or posture, seemed half-familiar . . . and the woman was her cousin. The man was holding her outstretched hand; when he turned to enter the car again the sun caught a wink of light from his glasses. There was the distant race of a motor and the black nose withdrew. Constance began to walk briskly up the road toward the house.

"Elizabeth? Oh, there you are. I thought you might have gone upstairs to lie down." Her cousin, coming in, wore a blown and almost young-girlish look that should have sat awkwardly on her big-boned efficient frame but was oddly attractive instead. Constance set about immediately to rectify it, tightening her rolled-back hair with severe fingers, removing the scarf that the wind had flung over one shoulder. She couldn't do anything about the pink look of — was it exhilaration?

She said, putting away her gloves, "It's a pity you can't get out today, Elizabeth, it's more like April than January. I don't know when I've enjoyed a walk more."

Elizabeth glanced across the room. She said casually, "Oh, did you walk?"

"Yes. I believe Oliver said it was almost a mile from town — but so pleasant on a day like this. Now" — Constance settled her glasses with a thoughtful expression — "I thought, for lunch . . ."

Elizabeth listened and didn't hear. She was jolted not so much by the gratuitous lie as by the briskly off-hand air with which Constance delivered it. It occurred to her for the first time that, out of appearance and manner and scraps of background, she had built a character for a woman she had never really known. . . .

Constance had evidently mentioned omelette and asparagus, because that was what appeared at lunch. Elizabeth ate obediently under her cousin's admonitions. "You must get your strength back, Elizabeth, and you can't do it on black coffee. It's not only for your own sake, you owe it to Oliver and the children. After all," said Constance, giving her keen attention to a roll, "you never know when you might need it."

The house quieted for Jeep's nap. Constance tiptoed upstairs for buttons to sew on a blouse; Noreen washed the dishes while Maire sat at the kitchen table and drew queer tripod-like creatures on yellow copy paper. Elizabeth took a shower and washed her hair.

She was brushing it dry when she heard Maire's long, mounting, infinitely chilling scream.

It caught her in a second's paralysis, locking her muscles, stopping her heart, striking her as incapable of movement as though it had been a bullet finding its mark. It echoed again, and sense and motion returned to Elizabeth. She dropped the hairbrush with a clatter and flung her bedroom door open and ran down the stairs. Like lightning against the dark she thought disconnectedly of Oliver saying, "Someday you'll trip, and break your neck . . ."

She reached the foot of the stairs and a peculiarly empty silence. She thrust open the door to the kitchen and looked in, her breath still catching harshly in her throat — at a scene of perfect serenity.

Noreen was drying the dishes, just visible through the narrow entrance to the pantry. Maire stood at the door, her back solemn with attention, her hands flattened against the panes. She was watching something, but nothing about her suggested fear. And yet, that dreadful long-drawn sound —

Elizabeth went quietly up to Maire and looked out the back door. On the sodden lawn at the foot of the steps, not ten inches apart, two cats faced each other in immemorial attitudes of fury. The grey one with scarred jowls shifted a trifle; his yellow adversary flattened its ears and howled.

Maire's cry, coming from a cat's throat.

At Elizabeth's side the child said absorbedly, "Those kitties in a rage, Mama?"

"Yes. As a matter of fact," said Elizabeth conversationally, "they're ouns, aren't they?"

Maire's gaze pivoted to hers. "Oun isn't here." It was half a statement, half a fearful question. The small hand reached confidently for Elizabeth's. "Look, Mama . . ."

She led Elizabeth into the living-room, stopping directly before the front windows; from her air of reassured triumph, she had been here moments ago. She said pleasedly, "See, there's no oun," and waited, her face turned up.

And Elizabeth stood there, more baffled than she had been before. She was sure, because of its singular echo, that Maire had borrowed her cry from a tom cat's howl. But she had showed no fear at the sight of the cats, so it was something else, some related memory. . . .

At a little after three o'clock, she went up to the studio. She found herself slipping out surreptitiously, which was ridiculous, because although Oliver had advised her pointedly not to, she hadn't promised one way or the other.

200

Nevertheless, she chose a time when Constance was upstairs to say hurriedly, "I'll be at the studio if you need me, Noreen," and made a rapid exit.

It was all wrong to feel this release in the little room on the top of the hill, but she did. When the light grew dull Elizabeth turned on the lamps, coming with a new freshness to her manuscript. The scene she'd ended on was all wrong. She hunted for cigarettes, found two aged ones in a package between the couch cushions and sat down at her typewriter to try another approach.

It worked, or partly; in the middle of it she discovered with dismay that she had used her last match. But if she could finish the chapter, she would have what amounted to a third of a book. She tried to concentrate, keeping her eyes away from the remaining cigarette, telling herself firmly that smoking couldn't be that necessary to her work.

She found that it could.

Regretfully, she gathered the scattered sheets from the couch, collected them in a neat and gratifying weighty pile and put them on top of her typewriter, slipped the cover over them and turned off the lamps. With luck, Constance wouldn't even know she had left the house — it hadn't been much more than an hour — and there would be no remonstrations from anybody.

There was no sign of Constance when she returned; her cousin was apparently still upstairs. Noreen said that Lucy Brent had called. "She seemed surprised that you were out at all, Mrs. March. She asked if you'd call her when you came in."

But Lucy didn't answer her phone, although Elizabeth let it ring for moments on end.

That was at four-thirty.

Darkness came, and a damp thrusting wind. Elizabeth forced herself upstairs to assemble clothes for the cleaner's weekly call; she would not have admitted to anyone her sudden and enormous fatigue. The radio beside Oliver's bed might help keep her awake; she turned out pockets, drowsily, and listened to a weather report that said there was snow and a cold wave on the way.

She crossed the room, Oliver's flannels over one arm, and sat down on the bed to turn off the radio.

Snow and a cold wave . . .

Better call the oil company . . .

How odd about Maire . . .

She fell asleep. She slept uneasily, half-conscious at moments of lamplight on her eyelids, too bound by lassitude to stir. She dreamed that someone walked up to her, someone close and trusted, but when the hand came out to greet hers it was not a hand at all under the cuff but an enormous paw with a bite of claws just under the fur. When she snatched her hand away — appalled, *knowing* — the familiar voice stopped chatting and ripped upward in a howl.

Elizabeth awoke with a jerk of terror. She had pushed Oliver's flannels violently away from her, but the scream still echoed on the air. . . .

This time it was Maire.

"No," said Elizabeth tensely to Noreen. "Let me . . ." She dropped down on her knees before the living-room windows so that her face was level with Maire's. She put her arms around the rigid body, hoping that the pound of her own heart would not communicate itself. "Show me where it is, darling, show me, and we'll make it go away —"

Maire went tighter. She said in a muffled whisper, *"Oun,"* and plunged her face into Elizabeth's throat, and Elizabeth, watching the darkness, turned all at once to ice.

There was a pair of eyes, looking in, watching. Yellowy and shining, like a monstrous cat's, just above the ragged black tops of the clipped-down cedars under the windows.

Elizabeth knelt there, frozen, her breath and her heartbeats afraid to move her own eyes from that blind and glittering stare.

It vanished suddenly. It was there, and then it was not.

Elizabeth only half heard Noreen's shaken release of breath behind her. She was watching incredulously as outside on the lawn a hand came up in salute, the blackness shifted, the porch light flickered on Steven Brent's face.

He hadn't been in the cedars — that was her changed perspective. He had halted on the path, probably struck by the tableau visible through the living-room windows, and the light had reflected on his glasses. . . .

Elizabeth rose, and gave Maire's shoulders a reassuring pat; her legs felt weak. She smiled at Noreen in relief — did her own face look as bleached, as sucked-dry with fear? — and said, "It's Mr. Brent." It seemed a long moment before the girl managed an answering smile and a murmur as she took Maire's hand. Then Elizabeth went to open the door.

" 'Oun?' . . . Oh, of course, the night we were here and Maire — Good Lord." Steven was concerned and apologetic, amused only when he found, five minutes later, that Maire would still come willingly to his knee. "What's it all about?"

Elizabeth told him about the snarling cats on the lawn that afternoon, and her own translation of it. The sound, probably heard by Maire for the first time at night; one of the cats jumping up on a window-sill to glare into the lighted room — "Something like that, anyway," said Elizabeth, and drew an enormous sighing breath, realizing the full measure of her relief.

Steven was watching her thoughtfully. He said, ignoring Maire's cordial invitation to exhibit his stomach, "You know, I think this has done you more good than all the medicine and rest in the world. Take a look in the mirror — you're a changed woman."

He stood up. "As a matter of fact, that's what I dropped by for — to see if you were well enough to start thinking about when we can expect the finished book."

He talked about dates and publishing schedules, and Elizabeth, naming a month that would give her leeway, went with him to the door. "Tell Lucy that I called her when she was out, will you, and that I'll probably see her tomorrow."

"I will. Meanwhile, I hope I've shaken off Maire's oun for good." He was smiling, but his eyes were intent. "Let me know if there's anything else, won't you Elizabeth?"

She should have been surprised at the

message behind that, but she wasn't. She had realized for some time that, of them all, Steven had caught an echo of the terror she lived with, without being aware of its cause. Her own instinctive ease with him had told her that. She said, matching his own lightness and the meaning behind it, "I might take you up on that some time."

"Good, do," said Steven, and was gone.

Elizabeth felt lighter than she had in weeks; it was as if Maire's monster, in crashing down, had revealed a doorway to safety and reason. She had been convinced that the oun was a synonym for evil, she had started up in panic at a child's aberration. That night on the stairs Maire had caught a glint from Lucy's lorgnette, or Constance's shell-rimmed glasses, or Steven's, and that was all there was to that.

In the kitchen, Maire's voice lifted in a peal of rage: "He ate it, he ATE it!" and there was a scuffle and a wail from Jeep. Elizabeth went in to find Noreen restoring order. Jeep wore a sated look in spite of his tears; he had managed to cram down most of two suppers while Noreen was stirring cocoa and Maire was in the living-room. Elizabeth gave Maire a slice of bread and jelly and Jeep a glance of straight-faced censure; it was difficult to restrain her own buoyancy.

206

The gilt clock said a few minutes after six, and she thought in a way she hadn't thought in weeks: Oliver's late. She would get out the ice for cocktails, and the anchovies and the imported crackers — it was, in a way obscure to everyone but herself, a night to celebrate. When Constance came in at the back door, returning from her usual before-dinner stroll, Elizabeth said at random, "Let's go out tonight, shall we? Have a drink here, and then find a place with no home cooking? We haven't been anywhere in so long."

Constance gave her a startled glance. "You oughtn't to go out —" she began doubtfully.

"But I feel wonderful. In fact, I —"

Elizabeth broke off short, her hands motionless on the ice tray. Behind her in the pantry, Constance said, "I still don't think . . ." and then urgently, at the quality of the silence, "Elizabeth! What is it?"

Elizabeth didn't answer. She stood without moving, head tilted a little, staring through the window at darkness that should have been absolute — and wasn't. She went on staring, until a hopeless trembling began and she stopped it fiercely, brushing past Constance, running blindly for the telephone.

# 16

She had thought in surprise, when she first saw the flaw of gold against the darkness of hill and sky, I left a light on in the studio after all.

And then she thought, But lamplight wouldn't — rush and ebb like that. It looks like . . . flames, it looks almost as if —

*The studio's on fire.*

It was like the plunge after a slow, icy, unwilling wade. Elizabeth lost a moment in sheer disbelief. Then she was on the telephone and giving the address to an alert voice at the wire, running into the darkness to watch the distant yellow leaping, not heeding Constance's wail: "Elizabeth! You mustn't, not without your coat, you'll catch pneumonia and there's nothing you can . . . Oh, Oliver, thank God you're here."

Oliver was a warm hard shape in the windy cold, holding her shoulders briefly, saying against her temple, "Thank God you're all right. When I heard the sirens heading this way —" The engines, arriving, blotted out his voice. A spotlight struck through the dark, there was a sudden noisy tangle of running men and fire hose.

"Put this on." Oliver was holding her coat; Elizabeth felt numbly for the sleeves. "And stay here, I'll be right back."

Elizabeth stayed, and watched the flicker on the hill as it slowed and dimmed. Her mind kept playing back her own cheerful voice, saying to Steven Brent not even an hour ago, "Well, let's see — I've roughly a third. Say about the end of March . . ."

But the weeks of work were all wiped out now, unless by some miracle the flames hadn't reached her typewriter. And the studio itself, the place of refuge, the only place in the world now where she was whole and intact. . . . Elizabeth dug her hands fiercely into her pockets and went on watching.

Beside her, although she hadn't heard her cousin come out of the house, Constance said hesitantly, "I can hardly believe it, Elizabeth, it's frightful. How do you suppose it started?"

"I don't know." Elizabeth had been too stunned to think about that yet; she turned her head and looked wonderingly up at the hilltop.

"They seem to have it under control," Constance said after a pause. "That's a

209

mercy, anyway. You keep a carbon of your manuscript, don't you, Elizabeth?"

"No," said Elizabeth between her teeth. "Like a fool, I do not." The hose was being wound back down the hillside now. The second engine departed with a roar. Elizabeth said, lifting her voice over it, "I'm going up to find Oliver, and see if they know . . ."

Oliver was standing just outside the studio, talking to one of the firemen. There were two others just inside the doorway, playing their flashlights over the soaked huddle of furniture inside. Elizabeth caught a glimpse of bare windows and blackened woodwork, couch cushions flung soddenly into a corner, the couch itself with a gaping hole in its centre.

The fireman, acknowledging introductions, said, "Too bad, ma'am. Nice little place here," and turned back to Oliver, apparently answering an earlier question. "Looks like it started from a cigarette between the couch cushions. You can see for yourself," he swept an arm back, "how the worst of the damage is right around that area. It might have smouldered out by itself, but with that pile of papers to catch on to . . ." He shrugged and, calling to the other men, departed.

With the lights and the voices gone, the studio was a forlorn, bitter-smelling little shell under the leafless trees. Oliver said, fumbling for the right tone, "Well, that's that. I'm afraid there's no doubt what the pile of papers was. Of all the lousy, villainous luck . . ."

Elizabeth shook off the light circle of his arm; with it went her own dazed, unquestioning acceptance. She ran into the studio, sure of her way among the damp acrid shadows, hearing Oliver call something about coming back later with a flashlight.

She didn't need lights, only her hands, carrying their own physical memory. And the cover of her typewriter, warm under her fingers but untouched by the fire and still fitted securely over the machine itself, told her everything she needed to know.

She was back at the house again, and the warmth and the cruelly mocking surface of safety, as though it were one of a million contented homes, and not — and not . . .

"You're cold," Oliver said, watching her. "Come over to the fire and finish that drink before we even think about this. . . . My God, what next?"

Cold, Elizabeth thought, lifting her glass docilely to her lips, not tasting what they touched; yes, but not a cold that bourbon or flaming driftwood could touch. She had just witnessed the beginning of violence. She had known it would come, because hatred was a thing that must be fed, but she had never faced it in such concrete terms as an approach after darkness, a match held to carefully placed paper, a silent withdrawal — to watch? Or merely to listen in triumph to the fire signal, the sirens?

Her outpost, the studio, was gone. Oliver had said, "What next?" — but how could you build barricades against a thing as sly and seeking as a mist, that permeated your very day-to-day existence under the name of deference, or loyalty, or love?

Noreen Delaney had been lingering uncertainly in the doorway while Oliver gave Constance a terse account of what the fireman had said. Now she took a decisive step forward, her young face worried. "Mrs. March, you're not well — you're shivering. Hadn't you better let me —"

Oliver turned sharply, Constance half-rose in concern. Elizabeth said steadily, stopping them all, "No. I'm perfectly all right, thanks, except that I'd like to say this. I've no way of proving it at the moment, but the studio was set on fire deliberately, after I left it this afternoon. It couldn't have happened otherwise."

In spite of her tight cool voice, it sounded preposterous, a defensive child's tale of masked men with guns who had broken the heirloom vase. Noreen lifted a startled hand to her cheek. Oliver, leaning against the mantel to light a cigarette, let the small flame die out between his fingers. Constance sat forward in her chair, peering over the rims of her glasses with a surprised and faintly affronted expression. Can she possibly, wondered Elizabeth wildly, be going to write a letter to the laundry about *this?*

The flicker of reaction lasted for perhaps five ticks of the gilt clock. Then Oliver struck another match and said in a conversational tone, "It's one of those things. Firemen are often guessing, have to be. The heater —"

"It wasn't on."

Elizabeth began to explain about finding herself in the studio with only two cigarettes, using her last match, searching without success for more. Unspoken, but louder in the room than her own desperately calm voice, were the things that all of them knew and none of them said: that Elizabeth without adequate cigarettes and matches was as unimaginable as a wingless bird, that when she was at her desk she would often, in her concentration, light a fresh cigarette while a forgotten one burned at a perilous tilt in her ashtray.

She looked at their faces. She said, "It isn't only that. I left my manuscript on top of the typewriter and put the cover over the whole

213

business. It isn't there — it's what the firemen found the remains of, on the couch. It didn't get there by itself, unless," said Elizabeth, suddenly tired and bitter, "the characters are more lifelike than I thought."

Constance breathed through her nose, a sign of distress and perplexity. Oliver propped an elbow on the mantel and looked into his glass. He said, "But are you certain —" and abandoned that as leading straight to trouble. "We'll go up in the morning and make sure. There's always the chance . . . ."

Elizabeth met his eyes, or tried to; Oliver's flickered away. She said, "I'll go and do something about dinner, if you think I'm to be trusted around the stove," and walked quickly out of the room, feeling the silence close behind her like a door.

The meat was overdone, the small green peas mushy, the potatoes past their delicate prime. Rebelliously, Elizabeth ate nothing at all. Oliver talked about a traffic accident in the Sumner Tunnel; Constance shook her head perfunctorily and began an anecdote of her own. Elizabeth nodded blankly at intervals and could not break out of the other world, the place of terror.

*Fire.* The hatred, bored and sated by the delicate vibrations it had set up in her life,

214

could feed for a time on this new and more personal excitement — the destruction of her book, the charring of her studio, the more subtle issue of her irresponsibility when alone, her need to be watched.

But this too would pall, and what then?

The children.

There might be a step between, but unless the evil were caught and stopped, it must certainly come to that. To Maire and Jeep, fast asleep upstairs, Maire with her pig within reach of her small relaxed hand, Jeep with the head of his fly-swatter protruding neatly from under the blankets. . . .

She mustn't think about this, not here, not now.

The thoughts came anyway, random, dreadful. The knife-rack in the kitchen. The medicine cabinet. The shelving of roof, with the apple tree leaning against it, under the children's window — such an easy swing up for an adult body, such a crippling plunge for a half-asleep child.

Elizabeth brought her hands up to her temples and pressed fiercely against the bones. Constance sampled the mint sauce and said consideringly, "Perhaps just a *thought* more vinegar?"

There were precautions to take and Elizabeth took them, walking stubbornly over the bewilderment and disapproval and silent concern that met her on all sides. The children's afternoon walks ceased; they played within the confines of the grounds. Elizabeth established a new regime under which, when the children had had their supper and bath, she heard their prayers and saw them into bed herself, inspecting their room and their windows in the process.

She went through the medicine cabinet and threw away paregoric, phenobarbital, the codeine left over from her attack of pleurisy: everything that might constitute danger to a child, or — at the very back of her mind — an adult.

Above all, she watched.

She watched Lucy Brent, who dropped in the day after the fire in the studio, full of horrified questions and headshakings; she watched Constance, whose long bland face might hide anything at all, and Noreen Delaney. She even watched Steven, whose wordless understanding had become a prop.

And, icily aware of the state to which she had come, she watched Oliver.

She thought, Which of them?

The children reacted instantly to the unaccustomed confinement and Elizabeth's new sharpness. Maire grew quarrelsome and mulish, losing her clear piping voice in a maddeningly accented sing-song with an expression to go with it; Jeep reverted to all-fours, said simply, "I baby," and behaved accordingly. That was why, on a bitter dark day toward the end of January when Noreen was off, Elizabeth gave the children an early supper and herded them up for their bath an hour ahead of time.

Here, at least, they were both under her eye. The water ran, the mirror and the window grew blind and steamy, wind rustled coldly about the shutters. Elizabeth pushed her white silk sleeves high, tossed boats and soap and rubber ducks into the tub, and caught herself straining for another sound over the tumult and splash from the faucet. But even when she turned it off and undressed the children absently, all her concentration on the empty house about her, there was nothing.

There couldn't be, of course, because Constance was out and the doors were locked. That distant click was the refrigerator, the muffled sound on the stairs was wood reacting to heat . . . and this was precisely what she was supposed to be feeling: that the bathroom, a refuge ten minutes ago, was in reality a trap.

The thought brought steadiness with it.

Elizabeth said, "Stop that!" to Maire, who had placed a dripping washcloth on Jeep's head, and knelt forward to intervene. She wasn't in time. Jeep, emerging from the cloth with his eyes screwed shut, flung a double handful of bath water at Maire, who leaped up in a stung-pink slipperiness that evaded Elizabeth's fingers, seized the towels from their rack and plunged them triumphantly at Jeep.

Elizabeth scooped them both promptly out of the tub and spanked them impartially; in an interval between howls she heard a door close somewhere on the same floor. Constance was back, and could bring her dry towels. She fixed the children with a bleak eye, said, "Don't move, either of you," and opened the bathroom door and stepped into the hall. She got as far as "Constance? Could you hand me —" before her voice died in her throat.

"Did I frighten you?"

Oliver was smiling at her. He took his shoulders away from the wall, breaking the terrifying immobility with which he had been standing when Elizabeth glanced up the hall. His face was watchful behind the smile, but it had lost its look of — was it rage?

"It was just — you're early, aren't you?" Elizabeth said it before she thought, because the finding of any words at all just then was an accomplishment.

Oliver's eyes changed. He said flatly, "Yes, a little," and started past her. Elizabeth was saved from speech by a violent splash from the bathroom behind her.

"Bad boy," said Maire with an undercurrent of admiration.

"Bad gel," said Jeep, complacent.

"Hand me a towel, would you, Oliver?" said Elizabeth, and escaped.

She dried the children and put them, suddenly meek and full of virtue, into their pyjamas. She tried to forget, because it was so disturbing, her first impression of a total stranger — waiting, menacing — who had spoken and smiled and turned into the man to whom she had been married for five years.

The children went thumping downstairs in search of Oliver. Elizabeth sat still on the edge of Maire's bed, recapturing in spite of herself the sound that had made her step out into the hall. It had been the closing of a door, and involved in it was the protesting shiver of faintly warped wood. There was only one door in the house that closed that way, and it was the door of Constance's room.

So that Oliver's early return from Boston, at a time when she would normally have been busy in the kitchen with the children's supper, was not as casual as he had tried to make it seem — was not, in view of his stormy face, casual at all.

What had he seen in her cousin's room — or searched for, and failed to find?

# 17

At ten-thirty that evening, because the silk scarf she had tied over her hair was wet with melted snowflakes, Elizabeth went reluctantly back into the house.

Oliver, deep in a book, glanced up and said, "Still snowing?" and went to the window to look. At the desk, pen poised over a sheet of notepaper half-covered with her small decisive writing, Constance lifted her head to say dutifully, "Jeep cried out a few minutes ago, and I went up. His head seemed a little warm, I thought. Do you think he might be catching cold?"

"Probably," said Elizabeth, and hung up her coat and scarf. "I'll go have a look."

Jeep was snuffling damply in his sleep. Elizabeth felt his forehead and the hand she could find; he was warm, but not alarmingly so. The morning would tell. She tucked in the covers and went downstairs again. Oliver had abandoned the window and was back with his book; Constance was sealing an envelope at the desk. Elizabeth paused a long moment in the hall at the foot of the stairs, and then found her voice.

"Isn't there — don't I smell something?"

Constance lifted her head, the light glimmering in her glasses, and sniffed thoughtfully. Oliver rose sharply to his feet. Elizabeth said hastily, "Not smoke."

Perfume. A tiny teasing whiff of it, as surprisingly present as a strange hat and coat draped over the newel post. It was a heavy scent, sweet, musk-laden, with a tired edge. It was the kind of scent that would be thoroughly at home in, perhaps, the Hotel Savoia. . . .

It was the scent that had hovered in Noreen Delaney's room, so palpably wrong in its surroundings, on the day an alien face had stared blindly up at Elizabeth's studio.

It didn't take her long to find the source. The hall closet door hadn't quite caught when she closed it, and the perfume was bolder when she swung it wide. Under her scarf, which had slithered to the closet floor, was a handkerchief, damp from contact with the wet silk, and reeking.

Constance wrinkled her nose as Elizabeth lifted it. "That isn't yours, is it, Elizabeth?"

The handkerchief bore no initials. Smoothed out, it was a small square of white linen, a woman's, but other than that, anonymous.

222

Whose fingers had dropped it, how long had it lain there before dampness had released the latent fumes?

To Elizabeth, it was suddenly the very smell and touch of hate. Aware of Oliver's grimace, she walked steadily to the hearth and dropped the handkerchief on to the smouldering logs. Behind her, Oliver was silent; Constance said startledly, "Oh! Did you have to — ?"

"Yes," said Elizabeth, and turned to face them both, her hands behind her back so that neither of them could see how desperately her fingers clutched each other. "I'll be glad to make restitution, but I happen to loathe that particular perfume. I think I'll go up now — is anyone else tired?"

Half an hour later, she gazed at Oliver's back, bare above the waist, and said carefully, "Oliver, I think I'll go away for a while."

There was nothing in her voice to suggest panic; it sounded like an idea she had considered for days rather than a desperate measure, thirty minutes old. But, watching Oliver's leanly muscled shoulders, Elizabeth thought that they tensed, as though his hands, exploring in his bureau drawer for a matching pyjama top, had forgotten what they searched for. If it happened at all it took the barest part of a second, because Oliver turned almost instantly and said emphatically, "Good idea — it's what you need. Get a complete rest from the house and the kids."

"I'd take them with me."

There was a brief silence, loud with the implications that brought Elizabeth's chin up defensively. Then Oliver said slowly, "Oh, I see. Where will you go?"

She hesitated only fractionally, but it was too long.

"You don't trust me, do you, Elizabeth?" Oliver was almost gentle. "My . . . God. While I — !" He moved with sudden controlled violence, shaking a cigarette from a package on the bureau, tossing the burned match in the direction of an ashtray. He didn't look at her.

Elizabeth sat up straight against her pillow, as stunned and tingling as though she had been struck. There could be no evasion now, even if she had wanted it. This time the small pause in the bedroom had the tight inevitability of the space between lightning and thunder. Into it she said steadily, "I think I'd better hear the rest of that."

"Do you? All right —" Oliver turned abruptly. Because his voice was as careful as hers, his face bleak and unreadable, the astounding question came at Elizabeth with no warning at all. "Where did you spend the night of November 19th?"

Incredibly, it wasn't a joke. Elizabeth stared at him. "The night of — here, of course, where I always do."

"Not that night. I was in New York for the stockholders' meeting. When I called home — late — you weren't here."

"Then I —" Elizabeth groped through bewilderment for a moment before she remembered. "I did sleep at the studio once when you were away. I suppose it was then. Constance must have told you when you phoned. . . ."

She looked at Oliver's face in the instant before he turned his shoulder, and the last words trailed away. The bewilderment went with them. Shock took its place, and a butterflying anger in her midriff. "Of course Constance told you," she said slowly, "and you don't believe either of us — which must mean you have a theory of your own. All right, Oliver, where *did* I spend the night of November 19th?"

Oliver's back had stayed grimly turned until then; the mockery stung him. "As a matter of fact, a number of people say you were at a hotel in Boston."

Elizabeth was so astonished that the full meaning of that didn't register at once. When it did it was like an answer in a crossword puzzle, radiating other answers in every direction. The Hotel Savoia and Oliver's presence there, the mysterious telephone calls, the menacing voice on the wire . . . but she must make sure of it. She said in a voice as impersonal as Oliver's, "The Hotel Savoia, wasn't it?"

"Yes."

"And not alone, needless to say."

"No — not alone."

In the silence after the short crossfire Elizabeth reached blindly for her robe, pulled it about her shoulders and slid out of bed. Oliver was standing furiously still across the room. She said incredulously, "You're paying blackmail for that — *blackmail*. You don't believe —"

"To hell with that." The violence left Oliver suddenly; he looked white and tired. "The point is that you make it so damnably hard —"

There might have been more; Elizabeth didn't hear it. She found her slippers and then the doorknob, and at last the refuge of the hall.

She woke at a little before six o'clock, stiff and cold, in the wing chair where she had finally fallen asleep. The lingering winter dark at the living-room windows, the silent yellow lamplight, the brimming ashtray at her elbow had a dreamlike air. With an effort, Elizabeth forced herself to face the inevitable waking of the house.

She emptied the ashtray, started the coffee, turned up the thermostat. She washed her face at the sink and paper-towelled it dry, and thought remotely how nice it would be if the shadows could be wiped away too. Tiptoeing like a thief, she searched for and found a comb and a spare lipstick, and when she had poured herself a cup of coffee in the kitchen there was nothing left to do but start remembering again.

Ugly as her own errand at the Savoia had been, Oliver's had been worse, because she had depended purely upon the evidence of her own senses and Oliver had not. He had gone there at the suggestion of someone else — not the person who hated her, that would be too dangerous, but a go-between — and he had found the evidence arranged for him. He had balanced that against all that he knew and had loved about her — and she had lost.

How?

Last night in their bedroom she had been wholly concerned with the repercussions between Oliver and herself; nothing had mattered at all beyond the fact that he could believe what he did. But there had been the solitary hours in the wing chair after that, and the realization that evidence of a sort would have been easy to supply after all.

There was her driver's licence, and there was the hair-colouring, the kind you could wash in, and, just as simply, out. Given even that vague assistance it shouldn't, at the Savoia, be difficult to find a clerk, a bellboy, to absorb and repeat a description of Elizabeth's coat, her bag, her rings — to cover a night when she hadn't been in the house, and Oliver had phoned from New York.

A woman, of course, would know the telling power of personal detail. And there had to have been a man.

Had Oliver also been furnished with a description of her supposed companion, or had he stopped short of listening to that? Put together, Elizabeth was bitterly certain, it would have added up to Steven Brent.

Go away now, today — the place on the Cape, the small house her parents had left her, hadn't been rented this year. She wouldn't have to see Oliver at all; she could call him at his office just before she left with the children.

Out of nowhere, watching the ashy dawn, Elizabeth wondered dully what people meant by a clean break. It wasn't clean, there were no neat edges at all, because you grew so far into someone else's life and possessed so much of his that it could only be a savage, rending affair. . .

Just as someone wanted it to be.

She found that, in making plans for departure, she had reckoned without Jeep. His eyes were drowsy that morning, his face flushed and hot. Elizabeth called the doctor and went stubbornly about the rest of her preparations, assembling blankets, warm clothes for herself and the children, a carton of emergency rations. She drove the car into Boston for a complete overhauling and a change to snow tyres, and then she prepared to wait.

She closed her eyes to the reactions around her: to Oliver's bitter, adamant silence and her cousin's speculation, to Noreen's troubled air and the shrewd curiosity Lucy Brent didn't try to conceal.

Deliberately, she locked herself away from them, allowing herself to feel nothing at all, until the morning of the day before she was to leave for the Cape. They were at breakfast when Oliver said abruptly, "Oh, by the way, I won't be home until late tonight. One of the vice-presidents and his wife are up from New York — Moulton was going to take them to dinner and the theatre, but he's home in bed and I'm stuck with them. So expect me when you see me —" He was rising.

Always, before, she and Oliver together had entertained the visiting hierarchy; it was an established custom. In spite of the iced neutrality between them now, Elizabeth was stung, so instantly that words slid to her tongue before she had time to think.

"I'm so glad you reminded me — I've got to dine out too, as a matter of fact. Crale, one of the men at Hornham's, wants to talk to me about resurrecting my book in time for September."

It wasn't true. Crale had mentioned dinner, but they hadn't got as far as dates. She had only to pick up her car at the garage in Boston and drive home again to dinner with Constance while Oliver, who had started thinking of her as an embarrassment to his work, did some deferential escorting of a vice-president and his wife. . . .

She caught a train to Boston at a little after three o'clock that afternoon.

She had regretted the childish subterfuge almost instantly that morning. Under Oliver's eyes she had felt compelled to go through with it, although it meant a sudden welter of rearrangements. A telephone call to Lucy, explaining that they would not be able to come for cocktails at the Brents' after all, apologies to Constance, who would have to curtail her activities as hostess at the charity bazaar in order to be back at the house by six o'clock, when Noreen Delaney had to leave.

But I'll be back by then, Elizabeth thought, watching the bleak marshes flicker by. I'll say Crale was called unexpectedly to New York, and Constance can go on being hostess and I can finish up the last of the packing.

At North Station, she took a taxi to the garage in Brookline. They were finishing up on her car, the foreman told her; they had had to install a new battery. If she could come back in about an hour . . .

Elizabeth found a small restaurant four blocks away and had a solitary cocktail and a chicken sandwich. It was nearly dark, at a few minutes after five, and a raw, raging wind had come up. She almost ran the distance back to the garage, coat skirts whipping, gloved hand anchoring her feathered felt cap.

Her car was ready, unaccustomedly shining, smoothly obedient when she pressed the starter. By this time tomorrow night she'd be getting supper for the children in the house at Orleans. Knowing that they were hidden and safe, feeling none of the sudden prickling nervousness that brought her foot down now on the accelerator.

She realized for the first time, with a sense of shock, how very close she had come to leaving the house unguarded for a dangerously long period of time.

It was night there, too, and the wind would be shaking the windows, driving the lilacs against the glass, meeting itself angrily around the house corners. And both Oliver and she were out of the way, for any purpose that might produce itself on a black and noisy night like this . . . the very eve of escape.

How could she have become so blinded by resentment at Oliver as to forget that?

The wind fought the small car, and twice Elizabeth had to swerve sharply in order to avoid toppled branches in the road. It was ten minutes after six when she went through the centre of the little town. Constance, barely arrived, would hardly have had time to change her clothes; she could go back to her hostessing. Elizabeth drew to a stop in front of the house as inwardly breathless as though she had finished a race.

She ran up the lawn under the toss and swish of maples. She pushed the front door shut on a shudder of wind, and called, "Constance? I'm back, so why don't you —"

But it was Lucy Brent on the stairs; it was Lucy, crisp, unfaltering Lucy who took that oddly fumbling step toward her, and spoke

232

her name in a voice Elizabeth wouldn't have known.

"What's the matter?" Elizabeth said, staring. "Lucy, what's . . . Are the children all right?"

How white and strange Lucy looked. How quiet the house was, as though two small and rebellious children hadn't been put to bed twenty minutes ago, as though there were only Lucy and herself here.

*As though* —

Lucy found a thin echo of her normal command. "Elizabeth, take it easy. Don't —"

But Elizabeth was already on the stairs and running.

# 18

Not nightmare, but fact — the waiting crib, the empty bed, the plush pig smiling foolishly at the dreadful silence.

Elizabeth went downstairs again, holding herself as quiet and calm as if she had discovered the children on a cliff-edge, where a sudden sound, an incautious gesture, would send them over.

Think, now. Before you pick up the telephone to call the police, think about what could have happened to Constance, to delay her. If one of the children had got hurt in any way, she would have had to take both to the doctor. Just because your children weren't in their beds at six-thirty on a black, wild February evening didn't mean they'd been kidnapped.

And even if they'd been kidnapped it didn't mean you'd never see them alive, or button them into their pyjamas, or spank or catch them close to you again.

On the other hand, if they *had* been kidnapped, it might be dangerous, even fatal, to call the police.

At that instant, Lucy said sharply, "Elizabeth!" and then, more gently, "Here, for heaven's sake, have a drink of your own bourbon, and don't look like that. There's been some mistake, the messages got mixed up. . . ."

"Messages?" said Elizabeth, and with the words she swam up to reality, and knew that she hadn't been there before but only existing in a merciful sub-layer. "Lucy, if you know anything at all about this —"

"There was a message for Constance," repeated Lucy, pausing in her nervous circling of the room, "at that damned bazaar. I got stuck as a sponsor, God knows why, and I was sitting beside Constance when one of the caterer's men came up to tell her she was wanted on the phone. It was somebody calling from the Touraine, she said, to say that *you*" — was Lucy's glance faintly inquiring? — "didn't feel well enough to drive home alone and would Constance please take a taxi into Boston and meet you as soon as possible. Like fools, we didn't check it in any way. We both thought —"

"I see." And, incredibly detached, Elizabeth did see: her behaviour of the last few weeks had seemed like the logical prelude to a crack-up. She said steadily, "The message wasn't from me, of course." Oh God, the moments going by. "So Constance left, arranging with Noreen — ?"

"No. Constance was in such a fluster that I said I'd come over and stay until you both got back, so she called Noreen and told her that. I got here at the dot of six, and I've been waiting ever since. They'll probably walk in now," said Lucy, forcedly brisk, "having been on some perfectly logical errand, and here we'll be, ten years older."

Neither of them believed it. Lucy's set face and wide worried eyes were a flat contradiction, and the faint repeated thundering of the wind said what Elizabeth could not bring herself to say: that no errand would keep Noreen out with two small children, one of them just over a bad cold, on a night like this.

While Constance, drawn away and disposed of by a false telephone message, sped in all innocence to Boston.

What to do?

To Elizabeth it seemed like a crisis she had tried to rehearse for at intervals ever since Maire had lain roaring in her bassinet. She would go to bed tired, furious, rebellious — and wake to think, What if I got up, now, and went into her room and the bassinet was empty? What would I ever do?

It had happened at last, and she knew she

had never had an answer.

Oliver would know, but Oliver wouldn't be home for hours, and she had no idea of where to reach him, unless —

Five desperate minutes went by at the telephone, with Lucy roaming nervously past her, before she found she could no longer stand the operator's leisurely connections, the paging at the hotels she called, the polite, faraway negatives.

Elizabeth looked at the clock, the cradled phone, the black windows. She thought clearly, This is what you're here for, this is the ultimate responsibility. She said, "I'll look upstairs and see if anything's — gone. Then I'll call the police."

"I'll try Steven again, he wasn't home when I called before. He might —"

Elizabeth lost the rest of that, she was running again up the stairs which she had descended, in some impossible measure of time, not quite fifteen minutes ago. She flung open the door of Noreen's room and switched on the lamp.

She hadn't quite liked sniping at the girl's cologne on the day an alien face had stared up at her out of this window; probing the small amount of privacy left to a household employee wasn't pleasant. She was ruthless now, throwing the closet door open, staring hard at the few dim shapes on hangers, gaze going instantly to a small suitcase on the floor at the back.

Had the suitcase been emptied?

It hadn't.

Downstairs, Lucy's voice said tensely, "—gone, both of them . . . What? Well, what else could it be? Get over here as fast as you can, will you?"

And Elizabeth stood staring at the open suitcase on the bed.

There was a beige cardigan and what looked like a nightgown, stockings rolled in a ball, a pair of black stilt-heeled pumps, very worn. Carefully folded away, a small cotton dress, flowered in peach and blue, still in the basting process.

A dress for a child of four, or five.

Elizabeth picked it up, half-numbed, and the child herself smiled up from the cheap blue rayon lining of the suitcase. Not pretty; a thin little face inside straight dark hair, with frightened eyes cancelling out the obedient curve of the mouth. Noreen Delaney, in miniature.

Not much older than Maire. . . .

But so very thin, so fragile. . . .

Elizabeth said softly, *"Oh, God,"* and slid a shaking hand once more into the cuff of rayon that lined the suitcase. Another photograph met her fingers, and she stared at it for a long moment before she knew that it was a photograph of Noreen.

Cool, deliberately flirtatious, a little bold; the eyes laughing, the vivid lips parted. A scrawl of ink in one corner said, "To Stony, from his N."

There were still the things she couldn't change: the shape of the face, the setting of the eyes. . . .

"I caught Steven in his shower, but he's coming right over," Lucy said. She looked exhausted. "He says — what's *that?*"

"She had a child," said Elizabeth, and said it again, carefully, while she looked for her coat. "She — had a child. Noreen."

"*Noreen?*"

Elizabeth found her coat and put it on; she glanced distractedly about for her pocketbook and saw it in the chair where she'd flung it, contents spilling out. She said to Lucy's staring face, "It'll save time if I bring her picture down to the police station — where are my keys. . . ."

Her lipstick had rolled, her cigarettes were tilting out across the striped cushion; there were all the familiar trappings of nightmare. Lucy cut through them with impatience. "I'll drive you, my car's here. But oughtn't we —"

"I'll leave a note, Constance might be back before we are, or Steven . . . there was a pencil here this morning . . . oh, God, I'd better bring pictures of the children too . . ."

"I have a pencil," said Lucy. "Go get the pictures, I'll write a note . . ."

*Noreen.*

So quiet, so very solicitous, with those small, deft hands. That air of almost pitiful innocence, the shadowed eyes that, Elizabeth realized now, could come from an excess of gaiety, a reckless spending of the emotions that must have been dammed and choked in this house. If you had a child of your own whom you couldn't acknowledge, and had to take care of other children, bathe their small satiny bodies, see the wealth of love and belonging they'd been born to . . . Lucy — shrewd, noticing Lucy — had sensed something false from the beginning. If only — but there wasn't time for that now.

Elizabeth managed to find one of the pictures they had taken under the tree at Christmas, with Maire looking seraphic for the camera and Jeep caressing his fly-swatter.

The fly-swatter. The pig . . . If she started to cry now it would be the undoing of everything, it would break through Lucy's layer of strength and she herself would go crashing.

Lucy said briefly, writing at the telephone

table, "Ready?"

"Yes. Let's leave the front door open, in case Steven, or Constance . . ."

She stood on the bottom step of the stairs, watching Lucy's fat little backhand that said with the haste of a telegram: "Constance — Children gone, out looking for them with Lucy. If you know anything call me at police station. Back soon."

Elizabeth watched with a kind of dreadful fascination while her own signature flowed out from under Lucy's pencil, sharply different from the script above. Forward-sloping, casually looped, as airy and expert as though Elizabeth herself had written it.

Lucy looked, too, and the pencil stopped on the tail of the "h" and dug sharply into the paper. There was a tiny explosion of breaking lead, and then their eyes, meeting slowly, locking.

Out of a kaleidoscope world, Elizabeth managed to say carefully, "Let's go, Lucy."

"Oh, no," said Lucy slowly. "Let's not." Her hand reached out; without taking her eyes from Elizabeth's face she crumpled the sheet of notepaper into her palm. She said almost casually, "We weren't going anyway, you know — no farther than my car."

241

The house shook under the wind, the gilt clock ticked. Elizabeth knew suddenly why Lucy's eyes had kept finding her face with such intensity ever since she had walked into the house. It hadn't been shock, or pity; it had been a devouring fascination.

She said, *"Where are my children, Lucy?"* and must have stepped off the stairs, because Lucy said sharply, "Stay where you are!"

The whip hand. The voice like a whip, too, flicking out, biting in. Before Elizabeth could move, it came curling at her again. "You're losing your husband," said Lucy stingingly. "If you don't want to lose your children too, you'll do as you're told."

She was shockingly the same, except for her tone and her bright unwinking eyes. Elizabeth knew dimly that she was all the more dangerous for that. She said as quietly as she could, holding back desperation, "What do you want, Lucy? Tell me and I'll —"

"Mrs. March," said Lucy, smooth and ugly, "will reach for her ever-present chequebook. Oh, I've watched you, Elizabeth, *how* I've watched you. Quite the lady of the manor, weren't you, when we'd go in to Bonwit's? You could write a cheque — and I could sit up for nights in a row, sewing at some dreary little copy. Clever Lucy, however do you do it?"

242

It might have been fantasy but for Maire and Jeep, and the wood of the newel post pressed against her shoulder. Elizabeth thought back in bewilderment to the other woman coaxing her on shopping trips, urging a blouse, a dinner skirt, a nightgown — and realized what a fierce enjoyment she must have derived from every purchase. Something else to feed into the fund of hate. . . .

She said wonderingly, "You tore the roses, didn't you, Lucy? And all the rest of it. I think you must be mad."

"Oh, do you," said Lucy mincingly. "I'm not, though. It's just that you had everything — and I had nothing. I thought I'd like to see how you looked wearing your world around your ears, that's all. It's hardly becoming" — Lucy cocked her head with indescribable malice — "but it's certainly — interesting."

The children, Elizabeth thought doggedly. Mustn't allow herself to forget the only thing that mattered. If Lucy wanted money, why didn't she —

But Lucy was staring at her, and saying curiously, "You never thought you'd want something you couldn't buy, did you, Elizabeth? Because you've always had everything. The clothes you wanted, the home you wanted, a husband so deaf and dumb and blind to anyone else that he only spoke to other women to consult them about you when you got home from the hospital. 'What shall we do about Elizabeth?' Never mind that you were all right, and the children were all right — just poor, dear Elizabeth. You lost a child, yes — but you had two others safe at home. Do you realize," said Lucy, suddenly shaking with rage, "that I was to come to the rescue — I, who'll never have a child at all?"

This was it. Far away — and how long ago? — Lucy's remembered voice said about a Christmas puppy, "We're to have the patter of four little feet instead of two, and something to tie Lucy down."

This was the seed of Lucy's hatred. Left alone, it mightn't have grown to the monstrous thing it was, but there was Oliver, whom Lucy must have wanted, and there was the symbol of the chequebook. Not the money itself, but the gesture; even now, standing in a controlled terror, Elizabeth knew that. No matter how classic the circumstances, Lucy could not be bought, could never have been bought. What she wanted of Elizabeth, what she had wanted all along with such terrible eagerness, was not her money but her destruction, complete, in a wiping out of love and sanity and safety.

And Elizabeth knew now what she had to do.

She moved, breaking the rigidity that seemed to have been a matter of hours rather than minutes. She couldn't see the telephone, but it was there, behind Lucy's thin, braced body. She said, "I'm going to call the police," and took a step forward.

Lucy moved too, but it was only the hand that had stayed behind her back while the other crumpled the note with the betraying forgery. She had been holding something that, while Elizabeth froze, took a slow, silver bit at the air.

Lucy had the kitchen scissors.

Shining, complicated things: you could cut spinach with them, or uncap bottles, or unscrew stubborn jar tops. You could sever a telephone wire with them very easily, or open a vein. Lucy must have gone for them as soon as she finished her call —

Her telephone call. Elizabeth made herself stop staring at the scissor points and looked at Lucy instead. "You're waiting for someone, aren't you, Lucy?"

"So are you."

"Who?"

Lucy laughed, a sharp, startling sound. "Who do you think?"

The back of Elizabeth's neck was wet. She said the name as she thought it, slowly, incredulously; "Steven?" and Lucy laughed again and said shortly, "You're more of a fool than I took you for."

The telephone rang. Elizabeth felt her heart catch and pause, and saw Lucy stiffen. It rang again, and it was all she could do to stay still, to go on watching and realize with a sudden quickening that if she had a chance at all, if the trap were not to close completely, it was this.

Because Lucy, in spite of her immobility, didn't like the loud, imperative summons either, or the things it had to mean — a hand holding a receiver somewhere, a voice waiting impatiently to speak, a wonderment growing in even the most casual mind, because houses containing two small children were rarely vacant at this hour of the night.

The telephone rang again, and Elizabeth steeled herself. If she could reach it before it stopped . . . Lucy's first peak of triumph was past; she was edgy now with the waiting and the delicate, dangerous balance between them. It showed in a flicker of pulse at one temple, a rigid stilling of her fingers so that the scissors pointed awkwardly in. She had been breathing fast and audibly before; she seemed now not to be breathing at all.

Gather your muscles, so very quietly, aim for that thin, strong, unmoving wrist. The whole manœuvre had to be a single uncoiling

246

action, or Lucy would be warned and the scissors might find her face.

The phone sounded once more — for the last time? Elizabeth took a final lightning look at that other face and felt every impulse in her body come to an astonished halt.

Lucy Brent seemed to have forgotten her existence. Her eyes, dark in the pallid high-boned face, had the huge, silent, swelling stare of a cat's. And she wasn't only watching. She was listening, filtering sounds out of the windy night. Elizabeth, who had heard only the roaring and oblivious silence of desperate concentration, listened too, gaze trained warily on the woman with the scissors.

That long, trembling scrape was the lilacs bowing against the windowpanes. The thump was a shutter, flung loose in the wind —

But the brief ringing peal, so close to Elizabeth that she jumped, was the doorbell.

*The doorbell.*

She knew later that one of the most difficult things she had ever done in her life was turn her back on Lucy and that dangerous stillness. That — waiting. As though, when she reached the front door after five or six running, interminable steps, she might let in another and horrifyingly familiar enemy — the person for whom Lucy waited.

She wrenched at the doorknob, and it protested — or did she sob? — and the door swung wide so suddenly that she swayed.

# 19

An enormous pink policeman, so like a policeman that he might have sprung from Elizabeth's own wild brain, stood on the step, holding his visor against the buffeting of the wind.

He said politely, "Mrs. March? We're just checking around — your husband called the station and asked us to. Has this man any business here?"

Elizabeth had her attention so riveted on his own rosy reassurance that it was an effort even to look away at the man anchored firmly beside and a little behind him. A stranger, neither young nor old, overcoated, felt-hatted, one of the thousands of people you passed and never saw. Completely anony-mous — or was he?

The policeman gave his catch an ungentle urge forward, and light from the hall reached ruddily out for the shadowed face. It caught the bold, curving planes of flesh, and shim-mered in the heavy glass lenses protecting his eyes. She had seen that face before, she had talked to it, had said, "I'm looking for Mr. or Mrs. Ambrose Miller," at a two-story house in Arlington.

She found her voice. She said shakily over the wind, "Officer, there's been a kidnapping here. This man and —"

Jagoe — his name came back to her in the instant before he spoke — had been staring coolly at her, as though daring recognition. Now he glanced over her shoulder, at Lucy. He said in the high, soft voice Elizabeth remembered, "You damned stupid fool. You —"

The policeman stopped him, after a blink of astonishment. He said to Elizabeth's wet face, "Just a minute, ma'am, what's that you said about a kidnapping?" and hoisted his captive briskly inside.

Elizabeth told him.

The words came out in a harsh tumble, further shaken by her glance at the gilt clock, and Lucy's voice, interrupting, was damning. "I don't know what to think, Officer, I'm utterly bewildered. Mrs. March has been ill, of course, and has been employing a nursemaid much too young for the job, who's simply taken off on some lark of her own and brought the children with her. As for this man —" Her

250

eyes roved with a remote and scornful air over Jagoe's face, the white socks just visible over his shoes, the stained pigskin gloves. "Is it necessary to say I've never seen him before?"

"Oh, you've never seen me before, Mrs. Lucy Brent." Jagoe's rage came out in a high, slow trickle. "Then I suppose you've never —"

Elizabeth was sickened by what came after that; the policeman listened until a shocked and incredulous scarlet overtook him and he said peremptorily, "Here, now! I'll call the station and report the children, Mrs. March, and then we'd better all go down and get the rights of this."

Elizabeth's ears still rang with Jagoe's detailed obscenity. She wanted, out of a mixture of rage and wonder and revolt, never to look at Lucy again; Lucy who had gone to the Hotel Savoia with this man, who — why had she never realized this before? — had deliberately registered them under the name of March, in Elizabeth's handwriting. That would be the evidence that had been shown to Oliver. . . .

But Lucy didn't matter now, except that she or Jagoe must be made to tell where the children were, because she couldn't stand much longer the peculiar torment that had begun inside her own head. It was a telescoping of all the years since Maire's birth, and a blending of her voice with Jeep's into a thin, lost-sounding cry. It was a condensation of panic and blind trust, calling, *"Mama,"* when she was unable to find or answer it.

The policeman started purposefully for the telephone. Elizabeth put her bowed head into her hands, pressing the heels of her palms in so that they hurt, and heard the front door open.

Oliver walked in.

His face was chalky, and grimmer than she had ever seen it, with a curious admixture of tenderness for Maire whom he carried still crying in his arms. He said over his shoulder to the policeman, "It's okay, skip it," but his eyes caught Elizabeth's and didn't leave them. Behind Oliver, Noreen Delaney was clutching Jeep. His cheeks were runnelled with tears, his fast-closed eyelids the only clean portions of his sleeping face.

Noreen moved gently with him. Her own eyes were wide and hollowed as she came across the room to where Elizabeth was standing and crying without any sound at all. She contrived the transfer of Jeep very deftly, so that he barely stirred when Elizabeth's arms came about him.

Maire stopped wailing at the sight of Elizabeth and the familiar room. She struggled higher in Oliver's arms, peering over his shoulder at the assembled faces — Lucy's in carven white ice, the policeman's, confusedly gaping. It was at Jagoe that she directed the unnerving, single-track stare of childhood before she said simply, "Oun, Daddy."

"He won't hurt you, baby. Believe me, he won't," said Oliver softly between his teeth. He didn't even glance at Jagoe; there was no one in the room for him but Elizabeth. He said almost lightly, "Speaking of which, did either of these — ?"

"No," said Elizabeth. "No, I'm all right."

She slid Jeep to her hip and reached for Maire's hand. She walked past Jagoe, she walked past Lucy, who flattened herself with a curiously feral movement. She heard the policeman say with desperate patience, "Mr. March, this man here —" and then she went on up the stairs to put the children to bed.

"But where *were* they?" said Elizabeth shakily, afterward. Her hands were still unreliable; she kept them tightly together in her lap, waiting for the reaction to go away. "I was half mad. I thought —"

"I took the children, Mrs. March." On the couch, Noreen Delaney lifted haggard eyes. "I never dreamed you'd be back in time to miss them, but when Miss Ives called and told me Mrs. Brent was coming over to stay with the children, I got — frightened. It seemed so funny, things working out like that when you and Mr. March were both in Boston. I didn't know what she might do if she got alone with the children, so I called a friend of mine, Rosemary Teale, and she came right over and drove us back to her place. We all stayed there until —"

Constance could stand it no longer; she interrupted in bewilderment, staring from face to face. "But I don't understand. What made Noreen suspect — ? Do you mean to say that she and Lucy Brent knew each other before?"

Lucy, a statuette, not glancing at any of them while she repeated her cool denials, had been allowed to go her own way. The policeman had left with Jagoe firmly in tow; Constance had arrived from Boston frantically worried because she had received no answer to her indignant telephone call from the Touraine.

She was waiting for a different answer now; they all were. Noreen Delaney glanced up from her hands, flushing. "I wasn't sure at first." The hands gripped each other, mutely defensive. "It was six years ago, in Boston. She wore her hair differently then and she wasn't so thin. Everyone called her Ceil — Ceil Poynter. It never occurred to me until I heard her called Lucy, here, that Ceil could be the other part of Lucille."

She braced herself visibly, gazing at Elizabeth. "I'm twenty-five, not twenty-two. My name isn't Delaney. I took that because —"

"I think I know," said Elizabeth gently, and Noreen glanced quickly away. "I was nineteen then, and working as a maid for some people named — but you don't care about that. They had a lot of money, and their son had just got engaged to Mrs. — Miss Poynter. We all knew his parents didn't like it, but they gave in. There were a lot of parties . . ."

Between the halting words, Ceil Poynter grew out of the lamplight, hungry, shrewd, fiercely determined under the air of sureness and casual poise. Her charm had carried her through the screen set up by cautious and elderly parents, and the conclusion was foregone: the sheltered young man, surrounded since college by suitable daughters of suitable families, was instantly dazzled. They had met at Christmas, they were to be married in July. But Ceil made the classic mistake of wanting the best of two conflicting worlds, and at a week-end house-party two months before the wedding, the worlds collided.

"I couldn't help it," said Noreen, flushing, "and I wasn't spying. I'd had the job of straightening out the living-room after they all went upstairs, and I woke up hours later wondering if there was something I'd forgotten to do. It worried me so that I went down to look, and — Ceil Poynter was there with a man."

She had screamed at the sudden, startled sound in the dark room, and the house awoke. The man with Ceil, whom she had introduced as a cousin, turned out to be a well-known figure in gambling circles — the heady world Ceil Poynter couldn't quite bring herself to leave entirely, whose stimulation she craved.

The affair was glossed over, the explanations of both parties accepted — and the engagement dissolved. For Ceil Poynter, the money and the servants, the summer house at Bar Harbour and the golden security of the inner circle, fled before a housemaid's scream.

Soon after that Noreen had left her position as a maid in the house. She left her aunt and uncle's home too, because she was going to have a baby.

She was not accepting the way out that Elizabeth had offered her. Her colour came up but her eyes didn't lower. "I hated being a maid, and he said he'd marry me. He didn't, of course. I'd saved some money, so I went to

New York and got a part-time job and had the baby there."

The baby was a girl, and frail. Noreen might have managed somehow to support a normally healthy child; she felt defeated before a long future of medicines, clinics, special care. She had made a few contacts at the dress shop where she worked, and one of them led to a home for the little girl. Then, torn between loss and relief, she had returned to Arlington to live with her aunt and uncle. (And, thought Elizabeth — remembering the gay girl in the photograph, looking now at the pale face and downcast eyes — the self-imposed sackcloth-and-ashes.)

The next time Noreen saw the woman she had known as Ceil Poynter was in Elizabeth's living-room.

She said again, "I wasn't sure. It was such a long time ago, and she didn't seem to recognize me at all. But there was something about the way she came in the day after Jeep's birthday. . . . I began to think who it was she reminded me of."

Of course, thought Elizabeth, her mind flashing back. Lucy in the doorway, Noreen at the foot of the stairs, looking at each other with that hostile awareness. And, later that day, Lucy's alien face staring out of Noreen's window, and the drench of heavy obvious perfume she would never have connected with Lucy, and the discovery of Mrs. Bennett's pocket-book on Noreen's closet shelf . . . would any of it ever have happened, would Lucy's bitter envy have overflowed the bounds of reason if she had not found the perfect scapegoat?

"She came to the house in Arlington," Noreen said, twisting her hands. "She knew I'd changed my name, and she guessed why — I suppose she'd watched me with Maire. That's where she met that — Jagoe. She pretended to be nice, she said she'd rather I didn't mention that other affair because it might get back to her husband, and he was so jealous. She asked about my baby, and said she wouldn't dream of telling you because that would be the end of my job. And then a few nights later, when you people were out, Mr. Jagoe came here to the house."

She shivered a little. "I'd always been afraid of him, and that night he told me that if I was careful and kept my mouth shut the way Mrs. Brent said, nothing would happen to Maire or Jeep. It frightened me, because he'd been outside the window long before I knew it — Maire saw him first."

Maire, and her oun. The very real touch of danger, pinpointed in those thick, curved lenses that watched among the cedars. Eliza-

258

beth stirred in her chair. Noreen said in a low voice, "Something else happened, later on. On Christmas day I got a telegram from the people who adopted my little girl. They'd promised to let me know if they decided to have the operation the doctors said she needed — but this was an emergency one. I couldn't think of anything else, I just left. When I came back I found that Jagoe had the name, and the address in New York. I must have left the telegram in the hall. I was so terrified at the idea of Mrs. Brent getting hold of it. . . ."

For the first time she began to show reaction, hands going to her cheeks in remembered dread. She said falteringly, "I didn't know what to do. I thought that maybe if I stayed and did as they told me, I'd be able to catch Mrs. Brent at something — because I could see by then that she was so jealous of you," her eyes went to Elizabeth, "that she hated you even more than she hated me."

"If you'd only come to us in the beginning —" That was Oliver, keeping his voice in check.

"Would you have believed me" — Noreen made a small, hopeless gesture — "if I'd made accusations with no proof at all about a very close friend of yours? When you'd never seen me before a few weeks ago — and I had a child you didn't know about and was using an assumed name?"

She said it quietly, forcing them to consider it. Oliver stared at the fire in silence; Constance, on the couch, shifted uneasily. Elizabeth remembered her rush of certainty earlier that evening when she had found the photograph of the child in Noreen's suitcase, and said slowly, "I don't know. I don't think so. . . ."

"I wonder — what about her child?" asked Constance awkwardly in the silence that followed the soft closing of Noreen's door upstairs.

Elizabeth shook her head, seeing again the small cotton dress on the girl's bed. Unfinished. She would ask tomorrow, because by tomorrow she would have room in her mind for something else beyond the indelible picture of Lucy, braced, vicious, holding the kitchen scissors. Had Lucy, waiting for Jagoe to arrive and turn to advantage the inexplicable absence of the children, intended merely to cut the telephone wire if it became necessary?

Or, if Elizabeth had struggled with her, would she have used the scissors in another way?

She would never know that, nor would

there ever be a firm base to her own conviction that Lucy, activated solely by her own destroying hatred, had allowed herself to be coaxed into a scheme for profit as well. With the stolen chequebook, the driver's licence, the hair dye, they wouldn't have had to use the ransom money until — something Jagoe had said in his rage came back to Elizabeth — they were safely away. The plan itself had been hurriedly contrived, forced by her own announcement of a trip to the Cape. Lucy couldn't allow her victim to leave the source of contamination, because peace and perspective might have undone all her slow and infinitely cunning work. She had gambled everything on tonight; that was why she had looked so white and brittle and unlike herself at Elizabeth's unexpected return. . . .

How very delicate the timing had been, how slender the margin of safety between Noreen's departure with the children and Lucy's arrival at the house. Elizabeth looked up at Oliver, who had reappeared with fresh drinks for all of them, and said, "What made you phone the police when you did?"

"I called here to say that if it was too late when I got rid of the Treadwells I'd stay in town. When I didn't get any answer — it was about a quarter to six — I waited ten minutes and tried again. I got thinking about the fire in the studio, and," said Oliver grimly, "I phoned the police here and turned the Treadwells over to poor Bishop and got into my car and drove like hell. It seems that the Teale girl — Noreen's friend — called my office when they got back to her apartment with the kids. They told her I was on my way home, so there they all were in the girl's car, half-frozen, waiting at the bridge."

The girl's car, waiting . . . something stirred in Elizabeth's mind, became the memory of a black car, the faintly familiar figure of a man, sun bouncing from his glasses — and Constance. She sent a quick, startled look at her cousin, and Constance was standing, playing nervously with a pin at her throat, clearly wanting to get something uttered and having trouble with it.

It came with a rush. "I suppose we'd better have something to eat — sandwiches, I thought," said Constance distractedly, and then, "No, let me . . . I did want to tell you both, though it seems such an odd time for it, that — that I'm going to be married to Horace Willett."

In the middle of their exclamations she escaped to the kitchen, blushing brilliantly, and Elizabeth swallowed an unsteady impulse to laughter. Aunt Kate's vigilance over the affections of her useful daughter had instilled a habit of secrecy in Constance, and the evasions, the mysterious exhilaration, the experiments with uplifted hair boiled down to nothing more sinister than Mr. Willett. No wonder his distant figure had seemed familiar; he was the rosy, prosperous owner of the market where Elizabeth dealt and where, for the past four months, Constance had shopped so diligently. . . .

But Constance had left the room, and she was suddenly alone with Oliver, and almost afraid to move and find that although Lucy was gone the glass wall was still there.

But if Lucy had built the wall, the hard, polished coldness between two people who loved each other, she herself had laid the groundwork. It had begun, she realized bewilderedly, with her own silent retreat in the hospital — and after that, when Lucy had started to make such skilful use of the emotional temperature of the house, she had walked arrogantly away from Oliver, putting more and more distance between them, expecting him to follow blindly and without question. And Oliver, stubborn, baffled, hurt beyond comprehension, had not. . . . Had Lucy left her mark after all?

Constance moved distantly about in the kitchen, and for Elizabeth, suddenly and enormously shy, it became the precious, seconds-counting absence of a chaperon. She said, "Oliver —" and Oliver said simultaneously, "I've been ninety kinds of a fool. . . . Exhibit A."

He came to the hearth to stand beside her, so close that Elizabeth had almost no attention to spare for the thing he held and was staring wryly down at, the thing that should have been surprising and wasn't. It was a registration card from the Hotel Savoia, dated November the 19th. Looping bluely across it, the casual, confident "Mr. and Mrs. Oliver March," in Lucy's expert forgery.

Elizabeth said in a whisper, "Jagoe had it with him?"

"Yes. . . . You'd have thought," said Oliver, "that I was trying to separate him from his right leg. He called for the law, but the law was conveniently on the telephone . . . Lucy, I take it? Or some homework of his own?"

"Lucy. But I don't see how he —"

"Jagoe used to be hotel detective at the Savoia. My guess is that he got thrown out because of a tendency to blackmail, but he still had an unofficial foot in the door. I haunted the place, asking questions, but they're all boys together at the Savoia."

They had had this to show Oliver, and she herself had shown him nothing but the unnatural moods of terror; she had flinched from the touch of his hands. She must have murmured something, because Oliver was looking at her and saying briefly, "The whole rotten business was like a magician's trick — hellishly convincing even when you know the rabbit's built-in. The trouble was," he glanced away, "that you didn't seem to be in shape to have a thing like this thrown at you. It wasn't until after the fire in the studio that I even began to suspect —"

"Constance. I know." Later, tomorrow, she would tell him about the cheques, and her own silencing doubts. She took the card from Oliver's fingers and dropped it on to the logs without speaking; it made a satisfying swallow of gold for the dying fire.

He still hadn't moved, or touched her. Elizabeth was queerly, painfully conscious of every breath he drew, of the faint brush of his sleeve against her arm, the utter stillness of them both. Then Oliver moved abruptly, turning so that he faced her. He said as though it were being dragged from him, "What about Steven Brent?"

Elizabeth stared. "Well — what about him?"

"I had an idea that you . . . that you and he —"

A full moment went by, in which Lucy, warped, triumphant, seemed to hover in the air between them. Then Elizabeth was safely in his arms, not knowing whether he had reached out for her or whether she had taken a single blind step; she was saying unsteadily against his cheek, "Oh, my sweet, how well she knew us both. . . ."

Footsteps echoed purposefully in the kitchen, a door opened. Oliver called, "Coming," in a voice recklessly full of ingratitude, and gathered Elizabeth closer and bent his head.

We hope you have enjoyed this Large Print book. Other Thorndike Press or Chivers Press Large Print books are available at your library or directly from the publishers.

For more information about current and up-coming titles, please call or write, without obligation, to:

Thorndike Press
P.O. Box 159
Thorndike, Maine 04986 USA
Tel. (800) 257-5157

OR

Chivers Press Limited
Windsor Bridge Road
Bath BA2 3AX
England
Tel. (0225) 335336

All our Large Print titles are designed for easy reading, and all our books are made to last.